FARRAR
STRAUS
GIROUX

THE WHISTLING TOILETS

RANDY
POWELL

THE Whistling Toilets

Farrar Straus Giroux
New York

Published simultaneously in Canada by HarperCollins*CanadaLtd*
Printed and bound in the United States of America
Designed by Lilian Rosenstreich
First edition, 1996

Library of Congress Cataloging-in-Publication Data
Powell, Randy.
The whistling toilets / Randy Powell. — 1st ed.
p.   cm.
[1. Tennis—Fiction.   2. Interpersonal relations—Fiction.]
I. Title.
PZ7.P8778Wh   1996   [Fic]—dc20   96-10475   CIP   AC

For Judy, always

THE WHISTLING TOILETS

1

IT HAD BEEN RAINING all day and I had to ride my bike home from my after-school job, which in eleven days would turn into my summer job. I wanted to make sure my mom saw how drenched I was. I found her in the kitchen boiling wieners. She looked surprised to see me.

"Hey. What're you doing here? You're supposed to be at the Forresters'."

"I know. Look at me. This is how wet you get when you have to ride your bike everywhere instead of having a—"

"Bus pass?" Mom said, smiling. "You'd better get changed and hurry over there. Bitsy just called. They're wondering where you are. She told me to remind you to *be sure* and bring those postcards."

"The postcards, yeah. Is Dad home yet? I'd kind of like him to see me, too."

"He's not home. Look, you're dripping on the floor. I'll tell him how soaked you were. I really don't think we need convincing, Stan. It's up to you to save for a decent car that won't leak oil all over the driveway. It's fine that you've chosen to coach tennis again this summer, but it really doesn't pay enough for you to — Oh, but look, you'd better get going, hon. And don't forget those postcards."

I went upstairs to my room. Talk about getting shot down. She was right, of course. That idiotic summer job hardly paid anything at all. I could have found something better, but for some reason I was coaching tennis to a bunch of runts at a decrepit neighborhood rec center.

The postcards. I'd had them yesterday, but where were they? Probably somewhere on my messy VIP shelf. My Shelf of Heroes. Let's see . . . there was a book by Vince Lombardi about his years as the Green Bay Packers' coach. There were two books by Arthur Ashe. Ashe hadn't been the greatest tennis player or Davis Cup coach of all time, but he was by far the classiest, and my biggest hero. My friend Ginny had given me his book *Days of Grace* two Christmases ago. I also had his earlier autobiography, *Advantage Ashe*, which he'd written in 1967 and which I'd read and reread lots of times. I had borrowed that book from my school library back in the fifth grade and hadn't gotten around to returning it.

Then there were my two special magazines. One had an article about an English tennis player named Lord Gerald Boxton. He wasn't a very good tennis player and he wasn't even a nice guy, but he was a wealthy international playboy who played professional tennis for kicks, and for that reason, he was a sort of hero to me. Also, I happened to be using one of his tennis rackets. He didn't know I was using it. It was the most expensive tennis racket in the world: the Derwint "Derbyshire" XQ-2R-200S. Made in England, the BMW of tennis rackets. I had acquired it two winters ago, when I was fourteen and working as a ball boy at a men's pro tournament in Seattle, where Boxton was playing.

The other magazine had an article about Ginny. It had come out in September, nine months ago, and since then I had looked at it so many times it was starting to get ragged.

It told about how Ginny was a rising tennis star, plundering the fourteen-and-under age division in several junior tournaments, rising steadily in the computer rankings.

The article also told about Ginny's personal tennis coach, Rick Donsprokken, who was the head pro at Ginny's club in Seattle and who also ran a prestigious summer tennis camp in eastern Washington.

A little over a year ago, Donsprokken had sent some of his best junior players, including Ginny, to live half the year at a tennis academy in Florida, where they would receive intensive tennis training and a decent academic education. Donsprokken didn't actually work at the tennis academy, but he knew the teachers and counted on them to keep his players in top form. A lot of personal coaches did this—sent their players off to an academy when they weren't competing in tournaments. That way, the player and coach could get a vacation from each other; the player could form friendships with other players and be exposed to different teaching styles; and the coach could continue earning a living at his or her local club. The other half of the year, Rick Donsprokken took his team around the country on the national junior tennis circuit, where the players competed in one tournament after another. "Team Donsprokken" had its own academic tutor, physical trainer, and sports psychologist. All funded by parents, financial backers, and sponsors who were betting that two or three of these players would someday hit fame and fortune in big-time tennis.

Ginny and I were neighbors. I had known her for ten years. I also knew Donsprokken well; I had gone to that tennis camp of his nine years in a row.

The article had a half-page color photograph of Ginny. She was standing on a sunny beach in Florida, wearing a sporty one-piece bathing suit with the brand name prominently displayed across the front of it. The clothing company had paid money to have Ginny wear its logo. The money went into the Team Donsprokken fund. Ginny got to keep the bathing suit.

There she was, with her thick honey-colored hair down over her shoulders, looking tanned and sort of kid-like. She wore a silver bracelet on her left wrist and a silver chain around her neck that had a small heart-shaped locket that contained a tiny photo of her cat, whose name was Boat. She was fourteen in that picture, but had turned fifteen in January, two weeks before I had turned sixteen.

"Stan!" My mom was calling from downstairs.

"Yeah! I'm hurrying."

I put the magazine back on the shelf. For a moment I'd forgotten what I was looking for. The postcards. Ginny had sent them in the mail last week. And now Ginny's parents had summoned me—along with the postcards—to their house for a meeting. Ginny's psychologist from Team Donsprokken was going to be there, too. Evidently, Ginny had mentioned to her psychologist that the postcards were "symbolic." I doubted Ginny would ever say something like that in seriousness, but her parents and psychologist thought otherwise. They were hoping the postcards contained some clue as to why Ginny had recently been on the skids and falling apart; why her behavior, both on and off the tennis court, had seemed vague and distant. But what did they think I had to do with it?

When I came downstairs, having found the postcards
and changed into dry clothes, my mom, who was still in
the kitchen, asked if she could see the postcards. I
showed them to her. She held them up, glancing from
one to the other, laughed, and shook her head.

"Do *you* think they're symbolic?" she asked.

"About as symbolic as those hot dogs. You ought
to grill them, to symbolize what's about to happen to
me."

"Oh, they're not going to grill you." Mom handed
the postcards back to me. "Roast you, maybe. Listen,
do you want hot dogs when you get home, or are you
going out tonight?"

"Both."

"Oh. That means you're going out with the other
two hot dogs."

"Just going to shoot pool, Mom. Didn't Bitsy say
anything to you about why they wanted to see me? I
get the feeling it's more than the postcards. They think
I have this influence over Ginny or something. Are
they going to try to pin something on me? I mean, am
I in trouble?"

My mom smiled. "I don't know. Should you be?"

I didn't answer. Deep down, who *didn't* feel like
they should be in some kind of trouble?

I left through the back door into the light Seattle
rain, straight for the woods. It wasn't the quickest way
to Ginny's house, but it was the most pleasant.

This evening the woods had a mossy, dripping smell. I must have walked down this path, who knows, maybe a thousand times over the past ten years.

Ginny and I used to stand underneath the trees, waiting for a single leaf to break loose so we could catch it as it zigzagged to earth. The path led down to a creek. We had seen salmon spawning, swimming upstream in six inches of water, their snouts long and green, their teeth sharp; they looked utterly exhausted but kept going.

Once we saw a muskrat carrying the head and torso of a Barbie doll in its mouth. Nobody believed us.

We had fished in the creek. One time Ginny had caught a small trout, too small to keep, but I couldn't get the hook out of its mouth; it had swallowed the bait and hook and everything and the hook was way down in its guts, and the more I pulled on the hook, the more I felt like I was yanking the fish's guts right up through its mouth. Ginny and I both panicked, but she was the one who started crying, even though I felt like it, too.

Coming out of the woods into Ginny's back yard, I walked around the side of the house to the front, where I noticed two workmen. One of them was digging a hole with a post-hole digger. The other was watching him dig the hole. The one watching gave me a brief nod and I nodded in return.

The guy using the post-hole digger had huge muscles, a deep suntan. He was sweating hard. His hair was tied in a ponytail, and a cigarette poked from his mouth. Nothing like having a smoke while you're doing back-breaking work.

I continued up the landscaped walkway to the front porch and rang the doorbell. The workmen's pickup truck was parked on the street, but there were two other strange cars in the Forresters' driveway. One of them must have been the psychologist's, but who belonged to the other one? Bitsy hadn't mentioned anybody else.

I was about to ring again, when the door opened.

"So you're the new housekeeper," I said.

"So you're the old Stan Claxton." Her voice sounded flat and bored. "Mr. and Mrs. Forrester told me about you."

She was young, twentyish, and, according to my mother, a grad student at the Bible college a few miles away. She wore khaki pants and Birkenstock sandals with thick white socks. She had an enormous ballooning rear end, frog lips, and glasses. She had pretty hands.

As she led me through the foyer to the parlor, I couldn't help thinking that if I were an international playboy like Gerald Boxton, this new housekeeper would have been sexy, with a body like the aerobics instructor at the rec center where I taught tennis, and she would glance at me over her shoulder and wink flirtatiously, and our wild and steamy summer would be under way. Ah, to live the life of Lord Gerald Boxton.

The parlor served as a waiting room to the den, where Dirk and Bitsy did a lot of business and received visitors. They were both wheeler-dealer types who'd made their own pile of money as well as inheriting some from dead relatives.

"What's with the workers out there?" I asked the housekeeper.

"Mrs. Forrester backed into one of the lampposts. The left one. Flattened it."

"What'd it do to her Jeep?"

"Minimal damage."

"Do you always call her Mrs. Forrester?"

"In front of visitors I do."

"I'm not really a—"

"I know what you are." She blinked several times. "I hope you don't mind waiting in the parlor."

"I bloody well do mind." I said this in my Gerald Boxton accent. Occasionally he took possession of me without warning. Kind of like I had taken possession of his Derwint "Derbyshire" XQ-2R-200S.

She closed her eyes in a silent groan. "That is perhaps the lamest British accent I've ever heard."

"What's your name?" I asked in my regular voice.

"Nancy. Mrs. Forrester will come get you when they're ready."

I looked at the closed door of the den. "How many in there?"

Nancy mentally counted. "Mm—five."

"Five! I thought it was just the psychologist. Who else?"

"You'll find out soon enough. Would you like something to drink?"

"Scotch-and-soda."

She closed her eyes again, that bored look, and repeated the question. I told her I'd settle for a glass of two-percent milk with ample heaps of Ovaltine. I watched her walk out of the room. That enormous butt.

I had always liked this parlor. Ginny and I had played many a board game in here—chess, Scrabble, Yahtzee, and Risk were our favorites. And one whole summer of practically nothing but Monopoly. The sun had a nice way of sneaking in very quietly and creeping across the carpet. But it was also a good room for standing at the window and watching the rain.

I checked to make sure Nancy was gone, then walked over to my longtime friend and partner, the Money Chair.

Good old Money Chair. I gave its green, smooth, expensive leather a few pats. It was an heirloom, Bitsy's side of the family. An inviting place for all those distinguished visitors to park their rumps while waiting for their power meetings with one of the Forresters.

I checked again to make sure Nancy wasn't coming, then sat down in the Money Chair. It made a pleasant sigh, like a weary dog curling up before a fire. It smelled like the pages of old library books. I slipped my left hand between the cushion and side and probed with my fingers, and began pulling things out. Dimes, nickels, quarters, two pens, a peppermint. I popped the peppermint into my mouth and counted the coins—$2.35—and dropped them into my hip pocket. And, to use the cliché, waited for God to strike me dead. Or at least to say something to my face. But God and I had not been on speaking terms for a while.

I sat and looked out the window at the rain falling, and heard one of the workmen out front cussing.

2

"I LIKE TO SEE young healthy boys drinking their milk."

Bitsy's voice gave me a start. I was facing the bay window, mid-sip in my Ovaltine.

"What do you think of the new housekeeper?" she asked.

"Nancy? She's great. Real abrupt."

"Yeah, she's pure no-nonsense. I wish I were more no-nonsense."

"You're pretty no-nonsense," I said.

"Only in limited areas. Just between you and me," Bitsy lowered her voice and checked over her shoulder, "she's kind of a know-it-all. Those Bible-college grad students usually are. At least the females. They're so defensive. But they make good housekeepers. As long as you don't try to tell them what to do or how to do it."

I hadn't seen Bitsy for several weeks, even though my parents saw her and Dirk quite often. Bitsy was short and what you might call pleasingly plump. Her nose was small and snubbed and usually sunburned. Her coppery hair came down each side of her face and flipped up into wing tips. Every visible inch of Bitsy was freckled, unlike Ginny, who turned a creamy peanut-butter brown in the sun and kept the freckles only over the bridge of her nose.

"Too bad about your lamppost," I said, following her into the den. My voice was tight and strained.

"Yeah," she said over her shoulder. "Bitsy was a bad girl. But I never *did* like those darn lampposts. They were Dirk's mother's."

"I didn't know you never liked Mother's lampposts." Dirk sounded hurt. He had grown up in this house. He and my dad had known each other as kids, and they were good friends now. On the surface they didn't have much in common. Dirk was pretty social, a suit-and-tie kind of guy, while my dad was a computer software engineer who wore T-shirts, tennis shoes, and corduroys to work. Dirk and my dad's friendship revolved around attending sporting events together—Seahawks, Sonics, Mariners, Huskies. Also music—they loved blues and bluegrass and jazz. And our two families used to go on skiing and camping trips together; we'd spent many three-day weekends at the Forresters' cabin in the north Cascades.

The den seemed very dark. Bitsy introduced me to the three other people in the room—a woman and two men. The woman was Dr. Teresa Ponti, the sports psychologist for Team Donsprokken. Dr. Ponti was very pretty, just as Ginny had described her in her letters—Italian-looking, large-eyed, large-breasted, soft-spoken. Her white teeth stood out against her olive complexion.

The two men sat tight-lipped, stiff, and grim in one corner of the room. I could tell they were money guys. Financial backers of Team Donsprokken. Why in the heck were *they* here? It had to be serious for them to show up. It had to mean their investment was in trouble. Their investment was Ginny.

Bitsy asked me to sit down in an armchair that faced the huge mahogany desk. She sat casually on top of the desk; Dirk and Dr. Ponti sat on the sofa, and the two money guys sat in straight-backed chairs. I gripped my Ovaltine but was disinclined to take a drink, not wanting to reveal my trembling hand.

"Did you bring the postcards?" Bitsy asked.

"Yeah, right here." Glad to have something specific to do, I pulled the two postcards from my back pocket and handed them to Bitsy. She glanced at them before handing them to Dr. Ponti, who put on a pair of reading glasses.

"Please keep in mind," Bitsy said to me, "our motive is not to pry. All we want to do is help Ginny. Okay? Will you remember that? Now, here's the deal, Stan. She's coming home in a couple of weeks. She's going to be playing in a tournament right here in Seattle. It's just a small-time tournament. Local girls, mostly. The minor leagues, you might say. None of the top players will be there, they'll all be at the Invitationals in St. Louis that same week. Oh, maybe a few decent players will show up. We know for a fact Kim Korticek is entering it. Ever hear of her?"

"No."

"You will. Anyway, Donsprokken and the rest of the team will be in St. Louis. But Ginny, the way she's been acting and playing lately, it would be a disaster to send her there. Her game is stale, her attitude is moody, her heart and mind seem to be somewhere else. She needs—we don't really know *what* she needs. Or wants. She thinks it might be a good idea to come home and play in a lesser tournament and fine-tune her game. Donsprokken agrees. He's entered her in the eighteen-and-under division. That's where Kim Korticek's entered, too."

Dirk spoke up. "Ginny really needs to turn things around, Stan. Show she still cares."

"Quite frankly," Bitsy said, "this just might be her last shot. Everyone's given her a lot of slack the past two or three months. Donsprokken's getting fed up with her. So are the sponsors and financial backers. They can't afford to have someone who's not produc-

ing. Donsprokken is considering dropping her from
the team. Needless to say, Stan, we're *extremely* worried about this. It's her whole future we're talking
about here. We'd like to get to the bottom of what's
going on with her. Dr. Ponti hasn't been able to. Dirk
and I haven't been able to. Donsprokken hasn't been
able to. That pretty much leaves . . . well, it leaves
you."

"Me?"

Dirk jumped in again. "You know how it is, Stan.
Ginny's not close to anybody. She really doesn't have
any friends—except you. You two go way back. So
we're thinking, you know, maybe she's told you something. Confided in you. She's having a heck of a tough
time, Stan. Going through a lot of changes—physical,
emotional. You know, turning fifteen and all that. And
heck, she's just come through spring." He laughed and
looked around the room, but no one else laughed.
"Spring, right? We all remember spring?"

"One thing we're sure it *isn't*," Bitsy said. "It's not
drugs. Donsprokken had her tested. It's part of the
routine. We're thinking—well, you know what she's
acting like? We're thinking she's—"

"Met a guy," Dirk said. "Fallen in love. Or some
variation of it. Has she mentioned anything in her letters to you? Meeting anyone?"

There was a long silence. I looked down at my
Ovaltine glass. Somehow it had gotten empty. The
peppermint in my mouth was the size of an aspirin.

My forehead felt hot and sweaty. God was getting me for the Money Chair, after all.

I shook my head. "No one."

Actually, the only boy she had mentioned in her letters was the twelve-year-old son of one of the host families she'd stayed with during a tournament. Occasionally, instead of staying in hotels, tournament players had to stay with a family, for home cooking and all that.

"We'd be sitting in the living room of this host family, the Trentwoods, watching TV," Ginny had written, "and that boy would stick his finger in his ear and dig out a huge chunk of copper-colored earwax on the tip of his finger and hold it out for his dog and call, 'Here, Deeter!' and Deeter would come trotting along and lick the gunk off his finger. Stan, when I saw that, I just about lost it all, I mean it."

I decided not to mention that.

Dr. Teresa Ponti, who was still wearing her glasses and holding the postcards, glanced up at me. "Stan? I've spent many hours talking with Ginny. She has a lot of respect and admiration for you. I don't know whether you know that. But she's confused. She's re-thinking a lot of things. She's looking for independence. She's off track—"

"Wheel in the ditch," Dirk said.

"I—I think these postcards shed a lot of light," Dr. Ponti said. "Thanks for bringing them."

I glanced down at the floor; then, for some reason,

over at the two gentlemen sitting against the wall. One of them crossed his legs. Both were eyeing me from behind their glasses.

"I'm not sure what you guys want me to do," I said to Bitsy.

"Help her," Bitsy said. "This tournament. Donsprokken's not going to be here, because he'll be in St. Louis with the rest of the team. Ginny needs a coach, someone who knows her game, to keep her on track, help settle her down. She wants you. You've always been good for her game. That's how she feels. Donsprokken likes the idea. And so do we. She needs a little pepping up. You're just the person for that."

I wanted to laugh. I did laugh. "Me?"

"Yes," Bitsy said. "You."

I held up my hands. "Hey, I—I'm not a coach."

Bitsy laughed. "Oh? What do you call what you do at the rec center?"

"Babysitting."

"I'm sure you underestimate yourself," Bitsy said. "But that doesn't really matter anyway. It's just this one tournament. Consider yourself a babysitter, if you want. Get her through this tournament. Help her get back on track. Be her coach, but also be her friend. See if you can find out what's bugging her. Not for the purpose of telling us, but to help her. That's all we want."

"We'll pay you for your time, of course," Dirk said.

"Just like we would a real—like we would any other coach."

There was more talking after that, but I was kind of dazed and wanted to leave. Eventually Dr. Ponti said that she was ready to comment on the postcards.

"These are really very significant," she said, leaning forward on the sofa. "This first one"—she held it up for all to see—"this woman all dolled up and marching in the parade. The parade symbolizes the pageant of life. Love, adventure, romance, the pursuit of happiness. Ginny wants to be that woman. She wants to be *in* the parade, not just on the sidelines, watching it pass her by. Ginny has always felt on the sidelines, never a real participant in life."

"Interesting," Dirk said, eyeing Dr. Ponti.

"The other one is even more complex," Dr. Ponti said. "A picture of a dog—one of those, um, wiener dogs—sitting inside a cowboy hat. The cowboy hat, broadly speaking, is symbolic of the various roles that Ginny assumes in life. The hats she wears, if you will—hardworking student at the tennis academy, teenager, rising tennis star, dutiful daughter, Donsprokken's pupil and team member, et cetera. All those roles are symbolized by the hat. You notice that the wiener dog is sitting *inside* the hat. Very significant."

One of the financial backers, who had not said a word, now cleared his throat and said, "Excuse me."

"Yes, Mr. Ross?" Dr. Ponti said.

"Are you saying the wiener dog represents a sexual organ?"

Dr. Ponti's face colored. "Well, Mr. Ross," she said gravely, "I really think we'd better just keep it on the wiener-dog level."

"Ah," Mr. Ross said, nodding. "Ah."

3

LATER, AFTER MY HOT-DOG dinner, I went over to Guballa's apartment complex and shot pool with Guballa and Wilcutts. Dan Guballa and his older brother shared an apartment because they didn't get along with their mother's live-in beau. Eugene Wilcutts lived in an elegant home on the shores of Lake Washington: his father was a dermatologist, his mother a dentist, and his two sisters bought clothes and tried on makeup and bras. Wilcutts and Guballa were both a few months closer to seventeen than I was, but they already had their own cars: Guballa's was a junker he'd bought with his own hard-earned money. Wilcutts's had been a birthday present; fourteen years newer and eight times more expensive than Guballa's. But Guballa's ran better.

Guballa and Wilcutts and I spent most of our time

shooting pool at Guballa's cabana. When we weren't doing that, we were driving around looking for a chance to do something heroic, such as foiling a 7-Eleven holdup or an attempted child abduction, or finding a carload of sexy women who wanted us to follow them to a wild party. In the meantime, we had conversations about specific girls, general girls' body parts, cars, or disputes about events that had happened during our elementary or junior high school days.

Tonight, we were playing eight ball. We always played eight ball.

Guballa had won his third game in a row, and it was Wilcutts's turn to challenge him. I sat down on the back of the sofa, which faced the TV, and tried to keep my balance without falling backward.

While Guballa and Wilcutts shot their game of eight ball, I told them about the powwow I'd just come from at Ginny's house. Guballa and Wilcutts knew Ginny, through me and through school. They listened with interest to all that I told them, and then asked me to describe, in detail, Dr. Ponti's breasts.

"With or without her shirt on?" I asked.

That stopped them for a second. Then Wilcutts leaned down and took his shot while Guballa crossed his muscular arms and asked, "Why would Ginny want you to be her coach?"

"I know her game," I said. "She can be very erratic

and skittish. Especially in the early rounds of a tournament. She needs someone who can settle her down. She's comfortable with me."

"You make her sound like a racehorse," Guballa said.

"What does a tennis coach do?" Wilcutts asked.

"During a match, not much. In fact, it's against the rules for a coach to even signal a player. But before and after matches, the coach does what you'd imagine a coach would do."

"Give thigh rubs?" Guballa asked.

Wilcutts still looked puzzled. "What do they want *you* to do, Stan?"

"Work with her. Take her to and from her matches. Help fine-tune her game. Find out if her game's really falling apart—and why. Help her turn it around—if she even *wants* to turn it around."

I listened to what I was saying. On one hand, it sounded like an awful lot. On the other hand, it didn't sound like much.

Wilcutts said, "Falling apart? She's not falling apart. You know what she's doing? She's asserting her identity by rebelling against her parents."

Guballa gave him a look. "Where the hell did you get that from, *The Brady Bunch*? She's not rebelling. It's the pressure that's getting to her. The traveling. The hotels and home stays. She can't hack it. That's the way it ends up with those child prodigies. They

peak early, then fizzle out. Can't keep up the intensity.
I'll bet old Ginny just wants to come home and lead
a normal, average life."

"No, no, no," Wilcutts said, tipping his head side-
ways and giving it quick little shakes. He had just
tapped the solid burgundy seven ball into the side
pocket and was chalking his cue and sizing up the
table for his next shot.

"What do you mean 'No, no, no'?" Guballa said.

"It's sex. It's gotta be sex. She's probably gotten
herself mixed up with some . . . some—what are you
looking at, Guballa?"

Guballa was leaning forward, staring deeply into
Wilcutts's face.

"Knock it off, Guballa," Wilcutts said, his eyes
shifting left and right.

"I was just wondering something," Guballa said.

Straightening up and leaning his cue stick against
the table, Wilcutts took out a handkerchief and blew
his nose into it. He was probably the last living person
under fifty on the West Coast who carried a handkerchief. And actually used it. I could tell he was trying
with all his might not to ask Guballa what Guballa was
"wondering." But Wilcutts would bite. He always bit.

"All right," Wilcutts finally said. "Go ahead and tell
me. What were you wondering, Guballa?"

"I was wondering what kind of drugs your parents
took to produce someone as ugly as you."

Wilcutts refolded his handkerchief and returned it

to his back pocket. Then he looked up and sniffed and said, "What was I saying? I was about to say something key. It's sex, that's it. She's probably gotten herself tangled up with some lucky tennis twerp. It's thrown her all out of whack."

Guballa actually gave this some thought while he watched Wilcutts continue to shoot. "You may be right. You may indeed be right. Maybe it's her tennis coach, Donsprokken. He's not married. He's got the stud looks. Yes, probably what's thrown Ginny off track is nothing but a tawdry, sleazy love affair. The old coach-pupil thing. Happens all the time, right, Stan?"

"You bet," I said. "Happens to me almost every day with my pupils."

"It almost always does boil down to sex," Guballa said. "Sex or drugs, and they ruled out drugs. So it's sex."

"That's what I said," Wilcutts said.

Guballa nodded. "Girl turns fifteen, it activates her—her gizmo. It's all Nature. Nature does all kinds of things to girls when they enter their child-bearing years."

"Gizmo," Wilcutts said, shaking his head and taking aim at the yellow one ball.

"I don't see her falling for a tennis twerp," I said.

"Okay, so it's a lifeguard or rock star or rodeo cowboy," Wilcutts said, sinking the one. "You meet all kinds at hotels."

"I think you need look no further than her tennis coach," Guballa said. "They do all that hanging out together. Traveling. Staying in hotels."

"It's not just the two of them," I said, trying to keep my voice level. "They're not alone *that* much. There's a team, a whole team. There's eight of them. They usually have to share rooms. Plus the full-time tutor and the trainer and Dr. Ponti, and the sponsors checking up on them."

"Doesn't matter," Guballa said. "A coach becomes a kind of god figure. It starts with some harmless flirting. Then some deep soulful conversations about life. And then, bam—they're all over each other."

Wilcutts finally missed, and Guballa was chalking his cue but seemed to be sizing me up instead of the table. "Stan, how about you tell us something right up front."

"Tell you what?"

Guballa stopped chalking. "You have the hots for Ginny?"

"What's that got to do with anything?"

"Oh, various things. It'll explain any strange behavior we see from you. It'll put things into perspective and simplify a whole lot. Think before you answer, Stan. Your answer does make a difference."

I stared off at the far wall. My first instinct was, of course, to skirt the question. But there was something coming to the surface. I didn't know what I was about to say, but I felt as though I needed to say it.

"How do you answer that?" I said. "How are you supposed to feel about somebody you've known all your life? Lived a few hundred feet from. Practically grew up with. We were both only-children. Our families went on a ski trip together almost every December. We went camping together, stayed at their cabin. Ginny and I spent six weeks every summer at Donsprokken's tennis camp. For a while we were mixed-doubles partners and even won some trophies. I've been writing her a lot this past year. I've always had good feelings about her. But the hots? I don't know about the hots. I don't know."

When I finished, I noticed Guballa and Wilcutts were looking at each other with mild astonishment. I don't know what kind of answer they had expected, but I don't think they had expected honesty. Neither had I.

4

"ALL RIGHT, YOU BUMS, line up!"

"We're not bums!"

"Line it up! Let's go!"

"How do you want us to—?"

"Calisthenic formation! Arm's length from the nit-wit next to you."

"We're not nitwits!"

"Shut up! Move it!"

"You said 'Shut up.' You're not suppos—"

"Can it!"

In the Stan Claxton book of coaching, there are four rules for handling runts on the first day of a new session:

1. *Be tough.* Glower. Chew gum. Put clobber in your voice.

2. *Keep them occupied.* An unoccupied runt is a potential catastrophe.

3. *Don't turn your back on them.* At least not until you have followed rule 4, which is:

4. *Wear festive underwear for the push-up demonstration.*

My two coaching heroes, Vince Lombardi and Arthur Ashe, would probably have agreed with the first three rules but would have scorned the fourth. But then, they'd never had to coach runts.

On this first day of the new session, it was pouring rain outside, which meant we had to meet in the gym. I was holding my clipboard under my left armpit and my tennis racket under my right armpit and trying to clap my hands, which made me feel like a seal. I was wearing my khaki extra-long-billed baseball cap, which reminded me of camping, because it smelled like the inside of a tent. I had it pulled down just above my eyes, to make me look meaner. Two pieces of sourapple bubble gum put a bulge in my cheek. My baggy T-shirt was untucked. My gray sweats were lopped off above the knees. Floppy socks, old tennis shoes, and the most expensive tennis racket in the world.

"Knock off the horseplay over there!" I growled. Horseplay. A true coach's word.

Somehow the runts stumbled into three rows of calisthenic formation, arms outstretched, fingertip to fingertip. Chomping my wad of gum, I surveyed the

troops. Pathetic. Enough to break your heart. Twenty-
three of them today, ages six to thirteen. Every na-
tionality. Rejects. Mostly new faces, but a few familiar
ones from the spring after-school classes.

"You pathetic bunch of beagles! You ragtag twee-
dleheads! Get down on that floor and give me
twenty!"

"Twenty what?" a girl in the third row whined.

"Push-ups! Anybody know what a push-up is? And
take off those coats! Why do you wear your coats in
the gym to play tennis? Everybody wearing a coat,
drop it on the floor! Now!"

Their security blankets. The ones wearing coats especially got to me, they looked so vulnerable.

A scrawny black kid with thick glasses and a hearing
aid raised his hand timidly. "What do we do with our
racket, sir?"

"Drop it on the floor!"

Another kid: "M-M-Mr. Claxton? I dint—I dint—
I don't mmagggot my racket today."

"Quiet!"

"But—"

"Relax! I've got extra rackets! Heaven forbid you'd
think of bringing a tennis racket to tennis practice." I
forced myself to keep a straight face. "Now everybody
shut your yaps. I want it quiet in here. I want it so
quiet," I lowered my voice to a rumble, "I want it so
quiet, so absolutely quiet, that if we stand here and

listen, we can hear the rain on the roof. Now ready? Listen."

Twenty-three runts stood still, heads cocked.

"I hear it!" someone said.

"Shhhhhhh!"

Silence. Rain tapping on the gym roof. A nice sound.

"Now," I said to my team, "I will demonstrate the proper way to do a push-up. Pay attention; I'm only going to do this once."

I dropped down to the floor. As I did so, I covertly undid the drawstring on my cutoff sweats. I did three push-ups—one, two, three. Then, standing back up, all I had to do was suck in my stomach. My pants slid to my ankles, revealing the brightly colored boxer shorts I'd put on for this first day of coaching.

The runts were silent for one moment of gaping, bug-eyed astonishment.

Then they started to laugh. They all laughed.

"What are you waiting for!" I yelled. "Start doing your push-ups!"

They just laughed. They laughed in a way that looked like they hadn't laughed all day and it felt good to laugh.

One of the girls pointed at me with one hand while keeping the other over her mouth, as if protecting it from germs. Her face was bright red.

"Your p-p—"

"What?"

"Your pants!"

Now the other kids were yelling, pointing at my pants puddled around my ankles.

"What about my pants?" I said.

"Look at them! Look at them!" a dorky guy yelled, jumping up and down, extending his left arm and pointing a bony finger. His right arm, I noticed, was a withered stump.

The Sour Lake Recreation Center was an old junior high that had been closed down a few years ago, taken over by the Seattle Parks Department, and converted into a hangout for senior citizens and what was left of the neighborhood kids, the ones whose families hadn't fled to the suburbs. Most of the classrooms had been locked up and boarded over, but one wing of classrooms, along with the gym, had been kept open and used by the community center for course offerings— anything from ceramics to Gamblers Anonymous to massage to tae kwon do to stamp collecting to how to get on *Wheel of Fortune*.

And tennis. Next to the playground and two softball fields were three tennis courts, two of which had nets. During the spring, I had taught beginning, intermediate, and advanced tennis after school. Now that summer had started, the program was called "Summer Tennis Camp." In addition to tennis instruction, once or twice a week Team Sour Lake would be getting together with other community centers around Seattle for matches—"exchanges," as they were called by some coaches. Most of these kids had nowhere else to be all summer.

On dry days I wheeled a ShopRite shopping cart full of dead, bald, dog-chewed tennis balls out to the tennis courts. On rainy days I wheeled it into the gym, where I simulated a tennis net by stringing a volleyball net three feet off the ground between two metal poles that were held up by tires filled with cement. On a rack underneath the shopping cart, I kept a blue canvas bag that contained a half dozen extra rackets.

We had to share the gym with the aerobics instructor, who held her Senior Workout in the northwest corner of the gym. The aerobics instructor had a beautiful body but a face like Humphrey Bogart. Which didn't necessarily mean she was ugly, just . . . weathered. She'd been teaching there for six months and I still couldn't figure out how old she was—somewhere between eighteen and forty-five. The sight of her jumping up and down clapping her hands in front of her and above her and behind her often threw me out of my coaching kilter. Her class usually consisted of about sixteen elderly ladies and a couple of men, flexing their spindly legs to show tunes such as "Oklahoma," "Mame," "Some Enchanted Evening," and oldies like "The Candy Man," "Bad, Bad Leroy Brown," and the theme song to *Hawaii Five-O*.

The hitting drills would be orderly for the first few minutes, the runts systematically taking turns, rotating. I'd stand on one side of the volleyball net feeding them balls and giving commands (and lots of praise). The balls skidded across the slick gym floor. Gradually things deteriorated. Balls shot to the ceiling. Kids fell down or got pushed down or were run over by the shopping cart. It was fun. When it got too noisy, the aerobics instructor would dance over to her boom box and good-naturedly turn up the volume.

If a tennis ball happened to roll into the aerobics camp, one of the elderly ladies would kick it back, hardly missing a beat of the music. Occasionally one of those ladies would give me a dirty look and shout in a quavery voice, "Young man, you are awfully mean to those children." To which I would shift the chaw of gum in my mouth and reply, "Ma'am, I'm not out to win no popularity contest." The lapse in grammar, I thought, gave me an air of competence and self-possession.

On the third day of the new session, another rainy day in the gym, I noticed that someone was standing in the far corner watching the practice. He might have been there a long time, though I only just now saw him. It was Rick Donsprokken.

I waved to him and told the runts to "carry on"

with their drills. I hurried over to him. We shook hands.

He gave me his easygoing, lopsided grin. "So this is what your parents shelled out all that hard-earned money for, eh, Stanley? All those years of tennis lessons and summer tennis camps?" He was in his mid-thirties and had shaggy dark hair with bangs. As usual, he looked like he hadn't shaved for five days.

"What in the heck are you doing here, Rick? I thought you were in Florida or St. Louis or somewhere."

"I had some business at the club and thought I'd take a little side trip and touch base with you. Ginny says hello, by the way."

"How is she?"

"Shaky."

I turned away for a second to watch the runts smacking balls around. Two of the six-year-olds had broken apart from the others and were sword-fighting with their rackets. I turned back to Donsprokken, who was saying, "It's getting serious, Stan. As much as I love that brat, if she doesn't turn things around, I'm gonna have to cut her loose. I can't afford somebody who's not giving a hundred percent. The backers and sponsors are already pressuring me to start looking for a replacement for her."

"What's her problem, Rick? Any idea?"

Donsprokken shook his head. "Sometimes I think she's just fed up with the whole thing. But I think there's something distracting her. Something's going on inside her. Maybe she'll spill it to you. Maybe it'll turn out she's got some guy she's fooling around with. I don't know. Maybe she's got a crush on somebody. You know, just between you and me—this is strictly confidential, now—sometimes I get this creepy feeling it's me she has a crush on. I don't know. I think she needs a friend. Somebody who can help her untangle herself and get herself out of this mess. You're the one. You always were good for old Ginny's game."

I shrugged. "In the early years maybe. She's done pretty well without me."

"She's not doing so hot now."

I turned back to my runts. "Hey! Owen and Abdul. You two knucklenoses better knock off the sword-fighting or I'll—"

"I'm not Owen no more. I'm Trandoor the Unmerciful. And this is Dry Repto-Goyd."

I shook my head. Donsprokken was chuckling. "You know what always intrigued me about your game, Stan? Your versatility. You were a chameleon. An impersonator. The way you could imitate almost any tennis style. It was uncanny. Trouble is, you never picked up your own style and developed it."

"I thought we were talking about Ginny," I said.

He smiled, keeping his eyes on me. "I was just reflecting. A guy can reflect, can't he? Okay, so, if you're going to coach Ginny through this tournament, you need to see to it she follows a certain regimen before each match. I've written down some instructions for you. Drills she needs to do, warm-ups before a match, nutrition; it's all right here." He handed me a spiral notebook. "Also, I wrote down the phone number of the tournament desk. Keep it in your wallet. You never know when you might need it."

"Thanks," I said. "I'll study the notebook."

"How long's it been since I've seen you, anyway?" he said. "Seems like it's been—you didn't come to tennis camp last summer. That was the first summer you missed since you were a tot. You realize that?"

"Yeah, but I had to work, Rick."

"Doing this?"

"Yeah. But I had another part-time job, too. Cleaning toilets."

Donsprokken laughed. "Somebody's gotta do it, I guess. But listen, Stan, you know something? I've been standing over there watching you for quite a while. You know what? You put these critters through their paces pretty well. You're a coach! I like your coaching style. Those kids out there, they like you. You're not easy on them. You remind me of me."

"Really? You're one of my models," I said.

He smiled. "Yeah? That's nice. Those kids are having fun. Heck, why shouldn't they have fun at that age, whacking tennis balls around? Listen, I've got a feel for people who have the coaching gift. I think you've got it. How would you like to work for me this summer? At my tennis camp."

I peered at him. "Doing what? Cleaning toilets?"

He laughed. "Coaching. Teaching. Most of my instructors are around twenty—you'd be a junior, an apprentice. What do they pay you here, minimum wage? I'll pay you three times that. Plus free room and board. And no rain in eastern Washington. What do you say? You know the camp well—the routine. You'd not only have an ideal summer job, you'd be learning a profession. Don't waste your talent at this place. How many times have I told you not to waste your talent? Did you ever listen to me? Nooo. Well, how about listening to old Donsprokken for once. Quit this job, coach Ginny through the tournament, help get her back on track, then pack your bags and come to my camp for the rest of the summer. What do you say?"

I told him it was a pretty tempting offer. But I hesitated. "Why?" I said.

"Why what?"

"Why me?"

"Like I just said. You're an old-timer at the camp. You're my kinda coach. You remind me of me. I need to groom a couple of apprentices. And you know what else? I like you. I always have. You do everything half-assed, but you're not a bad guy."

"Thanks," I said. "Thanks, Rick. Hey, listen, if you're serious . . . I'll take you up on it. I really appreciate it. I won't let you down."

We shook hands. It was unbelievable. I was stunned. Just like that, I'd accepted a job at Donsprokken's tennis camp. I'd been handed it. Did things like that happen?

After he left, I wanted to go off somewhere and catch my breath. But I had to finish my class.

Could it really be possible that in a few weeks I'd be an apprentice coach at Donsprokken's tennis camp? The very one Ginny and I had gone to for nine years?

True, a lot of the brats who went to that camp were rich kids from rich families, and yes, they could be pretty snobby and obnoxious. But they were normal. They didn't have defects or low IQ's or limps or fathers who belted them. Hell, they even spoke English. My runts would get along fine without me. Probably be glad to see me go.

And there would be my fellow counselors. College folks. The beautiful, the elite—the kind of people I had always looked up to. Those warm summer nights. When you were a kid there, you noticed it—something going on among the counselors. Romance, passion. You might glance out your window at midnight and see a guy and girl in shorts, sneaking off hand in hand. Occasionally, during dinner or something, you'd see a girl burst into tears or toss her glass of milk into a boy's face.

I was really going to be there this summer.

There was only one thing bothering me. It had come so easily. Nothing gets handed to you that easily, does it?

5

WHEN I TOLD MAGGIE, my supervisor at Sour Lake, about Donsprokken's offer, and that I had accepted it, she nodded somewhat gravely, added that she understood perfectly, and handed me a typed list of names and phone numbers. "Choose one," she said. It was a list of available substitutes for tennis.

On Friday, a couple of days after my conversation with Donsprokken, I arrived at Sour Lake to find that Terri the secretary had posted a telephone message on the glass windowpane of the office. It said: "Stan —Your mother called—Ginny here."

Oh. Or in the words of Lord Gerald Boxton, "Ah."

It was yet another rainy day. We were stuck in the gym again, and I was having a hard time paying attention to the runts. I was even having a hard time paying attention to the aerobics instructor's body. What was it going to be like seeing Ginny after a whole year? Why was I so nervous, excited, scared? I couldn't calm myself down.

I took a break from the runts and called my mother.

"You got my message?" she said. "Good. Ginny phoned as soon as she got in; nobody was here so she left a message on the answering machine. Are you going to stop and see her on your way home?"

"I don't know. I haven't—I haven't talked to her."

"Oh. You haven't called her yet? Are you going to call her?"

"Tonight? I don't—I don't know—I . . ."

There was a short, puzzled pause. "By the way," Mom said, "Guballa called about ten minutes ago. He said he and Wilcutts were coming by to pick you up tonight. Is that true?"

"Yeah. We'd already planned something."

"Then you're not going to see Ginny tonight."

"Well . . . I haven't—I don't know. Maybe I'll say hello to her but still go out with Guballa and Wilcutts. Like we planned."

"Huh." Mom paused, sighed. "Well," she said. "Hey, how about you bring her over here so Dad and I can say hello to her? We'd love to see her for five minutes. How about that?"

"Sure. If I see her. But I didn't say I was going to . . ."

"Stan? You okay, hon? Oh, now, look, it's okay to be nervous."

"Nervous—"

"Yes, about seeing Ginny. *You* know. When you're excited to see someone after a long time, it's normal to feel shy and inhibited, even reluctant to actually *see* them. That's normal. Don't worry. You two will be fine. Fine."

I hung up, seething and embarrassed. What was she talking like that for? She'd never talked like that before—like Ginny was my girlfriend or something. But I was mad at myself, too, for being afraid to call Ginny.

Back in the gym with the runts, I tried not to be in a bad mood, but there was something hanging over me. The aerobics instructor was wearing fluorescent-pink tights with a black leotard. We had chatted a few times over the past weeks, and now she smiled at me, which improved my mood considerably. When she finished her Senior Workout, she came over to me, smiling and sweaty, lugging her boom box.

"Hi," she said. "How's it going?"

"Making 'em sweat," I said.

"You and me both. You're a real slave driver. But the kids respect you. I can tell."

"Well," I said, "I subscribe to the Vince Lombardi coaching philosophy."

She kept her smile, nodding, but her face had

blanked over. It was obvious she had no idea who
Vince Lombardi was.

I didn't tell her I would soon be leaving. I didn't
tell my runts, either, that they were getting a replacement. I'd break it to them on Monday, my last day,
when the sub would be there. The runts were climbing the walls and I couldn't wait, to be rid of them.
Tomorrow I'd have to meet with the sub, Jeff somebody, to show him the ropes. Why in the heck did
these runts get to me so much? Why did they bother
to show up on rainy days? Why did they bother showing up for *life*?

I made it through practice and went out to my bike.
The rain was falling softly. I unlocked my bike but
lingered there, thinking, hesitating.

Okay, okay. Get it over with.

I went back into the office and dialed Ginny's number. I was out of breath. I kept clearing my throat.
The phone rang twice, three times. I got ready to
make my voice sound all enthusiastic and excited if
Ginny should answer. Put on the act.

Nancy the housekeeper answered on the fourth
ring.

"Hello, Stank Laxton here," I said. "Ginny
around?"

"Hello, Stank. No, but she left you a message. She's
gone over to the school to hit balls. She said you'd
know which school and what type of balls, and meet
her there if you can, she'll be there till about six."

I thanked her and hung up.

If I could just get this first meeting out of the way. This "reunion."

She'd been away a whole year at that tennis academy. More than a year, actually. Fifteen months.

How would Ginny have changed? Who knew what she'd be like now? What would I be like to her? Oh, knock it off, Claxton. Quit acting all fretful and neurotic. It's just Ginny. I had to be more detached and professional. Like a coach. After all, I was going to be *her* coach.

I rode my bike home and decided to leave it there and walk to the elementary school. It would buy me some more time. Also, having a bike emphasized my not having a car, which emphasized how immature I was.

It was a fifteen-minute walk to the school, but I stretched it to twenty. The rain fell softly on my face and dampened my hair. I came up over the crest of the hill and saw the one-story, flat-roofed elementary school—our old K through 6.

There she was.

I stopped and watched her from the hill. Wow. She looked good in her white shorts and purple pullover. Her white tennis shoes made her feet look big. She stood in the middle of the field, surrounded by a multitude of orange, white, and yellow golf balls.

She had always been a terrible golfer. Hitting golf balls was a sort of therapy for her. Find a big field and

whap golf balls and not care where they went. She
worked so hard to be good at tennis, keeping the ball
within the confines of perpendicular lines, that it was
relaxing for her to have something she didn't have to
work hard to be *bad* at.

I stood watching her. She had a smooth, rhythmic
swing but too much sway, and her stance wasn't
natural—she stuck out her butt. Balls were going
every which way, hooking onto the cement play yard,
slicing into the wooded ravine. Over the years, she'd
probably lost a thousand golf balls in those woods.

Well, Claxton, what are you waiting for? Go on
down and say hello. Face her.

For a moment I actually considered turning around
and walking home. Why should I seem so eager to see
her? Why not seem aloof and mysterious to her? Make
her think I had a life. A full, occupied, busy life, places
to be, dates with aerobics instructors. Make her wonder about *me* for a change.

Why did she want me as her coach?

Why was I acting like this?

The hell with it. Go say hello to her. Right now.

Actually, maybe I'd stall a little more. How about
walking around the field and down into the gully, to
the creek. More time to gather myself, gather courage.

That's what I did. Hid in the wooded gully. The
same gully, the same creek that separated Ginny's and
my houses a couple of miles from here.

There was a *tock* each time Ginny hit a golf ball.

In between the *tocks* there was silence. A breeze stirred the leaves; the sound of a squirrel scrabbling up a tree; the sound of my heart pounding. Light drizzle, wetter than mist, wetting everything. Then came the constant sound—my hearing must have screened it out—the gentle splashing of the creek.

Ginny and I used to do an experiment: Lie down on the ground a few feet from a creek. Close your eyes. Listen. At first the sound of the creek is faint, but it gets louder and louder. You get the uncomfortable feeling that the creek is inching closer to you, and after a while you open your eyes, just to make sure it isn't about to wash over you.

A golf ball came whiffling through the trees, ricocheted off two of them—*thuck-chock*—and the woods were still again.

I began hunting for golf balls.

It is pleasurable to hunt for golf balls when they're not your own. Looking for things isn't so bad when you don't care whether or not you find them. It's only when you really care about finding something and you're desperate and feeling pressure that the search isn't enjoyable.

I found an assortment of ditched items. An overturned shopping cart. A rusty NFL lunch pail, dented, with all the logos of the NFL teams from a few years ago. I opened the lid slowly, expecting to find a dead mouse or a severed finger, but the inside was empty and fairly clean and didn't even smell like bologna sandwiches. But it did have a familiar smell. It smelled like elementary school. I decided to keep the lunch pail.

I found a three-hole puncher belonging to Mrs. Bulmer, room 6, and a spelling paper belonging to Gordon DeCinces, room 4. Gordon had missed eighteen of twenty words. Whoa, Gordon.

I found a *Boy's Life* and a *Playboy*. Funny how two magazines with the word "boy" in their title could be so far apart.

I found two pens, two pencils, a red bicycle with training wheels, and a whole stack of *Wise Home Shopper* newspapers that some kid had decided to dump here rather than deliver to doorsteps. Good old Work Ethic.

Every now and then I found a golf ball, which I dropped in my pocket. When my pockets got full, I started filling the NFL lunch pail.

As if to remind me Ginny was still up there, a golf ball came hurtling toward me like a meteor and landed in the creek with a huge splash.

Meteoric. That was how that magazine article had described Ginny's tennis career.

I went to the spot where the golf-ball missile had splashed. It wasn't on the creek bottom. I moved downstream a ways and came to a pool, about three feet of still water. It was swarming with magnified golf balls. A veritable nest, a mother lode, of golf balls. I got down on my knees and started scooping them out of the water.

When I had scooped them all up, I climbed a path to the rough, where the field met the woods. Ginny was to my left, still knocking golf balls. Being a right-hander, she was facing me and noticed me. She waved. I waved back and started toward her.

6

I MUST HAVE LOOKED like a strange bird, coming out of the gully and trudging toward her carrying an NFL lunch pail, my pockets bulging with golf balls.

How to greet her. Something mature like a hug and a peck on the cheek? Like at some cocktail party. Beautiful to see you, babe. Mmwah.

She waved again, smiling. "Hey there!"

Her hair, I now noticed, was not only longer but parted on the side instead of down the middle. Her lips looked pink and soft. Mine felt dry and cracked.

"What club you using there?" I asked her. "Seven iron?"

"Six." She nodded at my lunch pail. "What you got there?"

"I bring you an offering from the ravine. A ravine offering."

Ginny laughed; it sounded slightly forced. "Let's see."

So much for the hug or suave peck on the cheek. I began spilling the contents of my pockets and lunch pail onto the ground around her feet. An offering indeed.

"I didn't hit all those down there today," she said.

"No, I stumbled on a—an accumulation from the past. Your swing looks good. Smooth as ever."

"Lotta good it does me."

"Yeah, seems like you've gotten worse, if that's possible."

"It's possible."

There was an almost unbearable five seconds during which it seemed we had run out of things to say.

"I hope I didn't hit any squirrels," she said.

I grunted, unable to think of a reply.

"How come you were in the gully?" she asked.

"Oh . . . gathering golf balls." My eyes met hers for a half second. Hers had a gleam that said she didn't buy my answer; that she suspected I'd been down in the gully gathering something other than golf balls.

"Find anything interesting down there?" she asked.

"Down there? Oh, you'd be surprised."

"Condoms," she said.

"What?"

"Oh, I just—I guessed there'd be—" Her cheeks went pink.

"Oh," I said, nodding and looking off at the woods. "That's a good guess. Yeah, you'd think there'd be—a few of those. Used, of course. I didn't—uh—where'd you fly in from today?"

"Well, let's see . . . Dallas. When I left the academy I flew to Dallas."

"You flew here from Dallas?"

"Yes. Well, I stayed a couple nights in Dallas, outside of Dallas, with a family I know. Two sons, two daughters, two parents, some horses, a swimming pool, and they're all tennis nuts."

I nodded, taking this in, processing it. A strange coldness crept into my stomach. Two sons. Dallas. Cowboy hat. Wiener dog. Hm.

"Still have your Lord Boxton racket?" she asked.

"Of course I still have it," I said. "Why wouldn't I still have it? Of course I do."

Ginny looked amused. "Sorry. Just asking."

"What was that you were saying about squirrels?" I said.

"Squirrels?"

"You were hoping you hadn't hit any in the gully."

"Yeah," Ginny said. "Don't you remember about the squirrels? That camping trip we went on where our parents rented the Winnebago? We drove to eastern Washington, stayed at that campground at Moses Lake. You and I went hiking up the trails and threw rocks down below, and that crazy girl came running out of nowhere all blubbering and hysterical, saying we'd hit a squirrel in the eye."

"I remember," I said, nodding. "She was psycho."

"Or pretending to be," Ginny said. "It seemed like people at that campground did all sorts of things like that."

I had no idea what she meant by that, but I let it go. "I remember it clearly now," I said. "In fact, it's about the only thing from that Winnebago trip I do remember, except your dad yelling at us for reading *Mad* magazines instead of looking at the scenery."

"And your dad wanting to stop and get a licorice milk shake, but your mom kept saying, 'You don't *need* a licorice milk shake,' and your dad yelling, 'Of course I don't *need* a licorice milk shake, nobody *needs* a licorice milk shake.' "

We laughed. "I think you and I were the only ones who didn't argue on that trip," I said.

"Remember that other place we stayed, after Moses Lake?" she said. "It was another state park. There were some fraternity guys playing tackle football at the picnic grounds. Some of them had taken their shirts off. The guy who was playing quarterback, he took off his shirt and I—I turned to you—we were both watching the game—and I said, 'Stan, that guy has breasts!' And you started laughing. You said, 'You dope, those are his *muscles*. He's just got really developed pecs.' I'll never forget that. I was eight years old. I was so embarrassed." She paused. "Would you like to hit some?"

"Sure."

"You can use my seven iron and I'll keep the six. Let's aim into the gully."

"What, on purpose?"

She smiled and tilted her head. "And after you just went around and picked up all those goff balls."

Ginny had an annoying way of leaving the *l* off the word "golf" and pronouncing it "goff." She must have done it on purpose; it was the only word she mispronounced. Someday when we had nothing else in the world to talk about, I would ask her if she had any particular reason for mispronouncing it, and if not, then how about stopping it, since it kind of bugged me.

"We won't really hit a squirrel, will we?" she asked.

"Only the ones who deserve it," I said.

We knocked a few balls into the ravine, but I stopped. "Ginny, I can't bring myself to lose perfectly good golf balls."

"Oh, all right. You've grown a conscience this past year, eh? Okay, let's aim over there for those monkey bars. One point if you hit them on the bounce and two points if you hit them on the fly."

Ever the competitor. We hit for the monkey bars. Her sleeves were rolled up and her arms were long and slender and tanned, with short blond hairs. Her right arm was more developed than her left.

We were both racking up points.

"You sure get good loft with that six iron," I said. "You really get under them."

"Yep." She whacked another golf ball and I watched it fly toward the custodian's office. Her looped earrings tapped the downy spot between her neck and jawbone.

After we had hit all the golf balls, we walked around picking them up and replacing our divots. It had stopped drizzling. The sky was changing from afternoon to evening.

"Got something planned tonight?" she asked.

"Oh, yeah," I said, trying to make it sound like I had about thirteen things to choose from.

"Like what?" she asked.

"I'm going out with Guballa and Wilcutts."

"How are those two?"

"As unchanged as two people can possibly be."

"Do they have girlfriends yet?"

"Like I said, as unchanged as two people can—"

"What about you?" she asked.

"What, am I changed?"

"Got a girl yet."

I hesitated. Her voice had sounded almost too . . . casual. "If I did I wouldn't be going out with Guballa and Wilcutts. Besides, I would have written you about it. I tell you, though, Ginny. Things seem to be moving in that department."

"Moving?"

"Lately I've had some pretty bizarre encounters with girls."

"Really? Can I hear?"

So I told her while we collected golf balls. I told her first about the aerobics instructor at Sour Lake, about how I had been thinking of asking her out but was reluctant to before I pinned down her age. "And now I find out she's never heard of Vince Lombardi," I said.

Then I told her about how one of my runts, a seventh-grader, had invited me to her birthday party back in April. And I had *gone*. I had *gone* to her birthday party in April, and I couldn't for the life of me explain why she had invited me or why I had accepted. When I arrived at the party, seven girls wearing party dresses were sitting around the dining-room table, giggling. And there I was. Her tennis coach. I stayed for fifteen minutes. Then I got up abruptly and said I suddenly remembered I had a dentist appointment. She quit coming to tennis. I never saw her again.

"How sad," Ginny said, looking away. "She must've had a crush on you. That happened in April? You didn't write me about that."

"Didn't I? No, I guess I was still . . . processing it. But wait, I haven't even gotten to the most bizarre encounter of all. This one's been giving me nightmares. Daymares, too."

"I can't wait."

I told her about the pinch and the pornographic gesture.

The pinch had happened in the semi-crowded hallway at school between third and fourth periods, while I was spinning the combination of my locker. Something pinched my left buttock—incredibly strong fingers. The girl who had done it had simply continued walking past me down the hall, not turning around, her brown frizzy hair bouncing behind her. She had not worn a bra for eight straight school days. I had been keeping count. Evidently she had noticed me keeping count, noticed me eyeing her joggling pointers, and had delivered a message: Quit gawking, you boob.

"At least," I told Ginny, "I guess that was the message. You don't think it could have been some weird come-on, do you?"

"It's possible," Ginny said. "I mean, she did use her fingers. It's not like she used pliers or something."

"But wait," I said. "That's only the first half of it. Three days later, I'm riding my bike down the street, on my way to Sour Lake. Riding through one of the shabbiest neighborhoods. Usually I avoid it, but for some reason I took that route that day."

Coasting along on my rickety Schwinn, past boxlike houses, front yards with mongrels or old mattresses or refrigerators or broken-down cars on blocks, I had come to a yellow house with a white picket fence. And there, standing in the front yard, was the girl who had pinched me. Looking chubby in her tight cutoffs and halter top. Just standing in her front yard, not taking her eyes off me. And I—I couldn't stop looking back at her. Her ruddy, pimpled face showed no expression. The hairs on the back of my neck prickled. My body felt quivery and jumpy. There was a dull ache on my left buttock where she had pinched it the other day. My blood fizzed.

Then she calmly turned her back to me, bent over, and, looking at me upside down from between her legs, flipped me off.

I shimmied and teetered and tottered on my bike, but regained control—while she kept making the gesture—and hurried down the street.

"Well," Ginny said. "I think *that* might be a come-on."

"You think so?"

"Yeah," she said, "but you should ask Guballa. He'd know."

"He'd want her address," I said. "But I'm sure not going to pursue it."

"No?"

"No way."

"It reminds me of a book I've read five or six times," Ginny said. "An old classic called *The Moffats*. The main character, every once in a while, she bends over to look at the world 'the upside-down way.' Everything has a brighter, fresher look. The blue sky, the puffy clouds, the green grass, the houses on the other side of the street, the picket fences—the whole world clean and pure. Ever try it?" Ginny bent over. Her hair spilled to the ground.

"Grab that divot while you're down there," I said. "Guballa once said that replacing your divots is the highest form of morality."

"Speaking of classics," Ginny said, still bending over, "your letters were great. I took them everywhere. They were *you*."

"Glad you liked them," I said, feeling embarrassed but proud. "I mostly just winged it."

"You're good at that," she said. "Hey, Stan?"

"Yeah?"

"Are you glad I'm here?"

"Hell no."

She made a face, but I got confused whether it was a smile or a frown, because she was still upside-down. Finally, she straightened up and shook her hair. I asked her if she'd like to come back and say hello to my folks. She said she'd like that.

We started walking back. I played the gentleman and carried her clubs and ball bag; she carried my empty lunch pail.

"It smells so familiar around here," Ginny said, and she smiled with her mouth closed, as if she were inhaling. "I've missed that sweet piney smell. Other places have nice smells, but not quite like that—that piney smell."

"Must be the pines," I said.

She said, "I must've thought a hundred times this past year about going up to the cabin. Just holing up there for a week or ten days and taking a different hike every day."

"No wonder your tennis stinks," I said. She said nothing. "Why *are* you here, Ginny?"

"What's everyone told you?"

She knew about my meeting with her folks and Dr. Ponti and the two other men. She also knew I'd seen Donsprokken. "That you're here for the tournament. But I'm not sure whether it's to fine-tune your game or—or to salvage it."

"What else did they say?"

"Oh, they made a lot of metaphors, like you have a wheel in the ditch and you're going through rough waters. You're on the skids. Falling apart. Throwing everything away. Breaking down. Coming unglued. Is that how you see it?"

"A machine gone haywire, huh?" she said.

"No, not entirely a machine," I said. "Your parents, they—uh—also were thinking that maybe you've gotten distracted by a romance or something. You've flipped out for some guy that you haven't told anyone about. Or maybe have a crush on some guy. Donsprokken thinks that, too."

She showed no reaction, except a raising of the eyebrows and a quick flaring of the nostrils.

"Shows where *their* minds are at," she said. "Sheesh, they *would* think that."

"What, you mean sex? That's what it usually boils down to," I said, stealing Guballa's line.

"Does it really?" Ginny said. "Is that how much credit you give a person? What, their whole life and future, the choices they make, all based on physical gratification?"

"Yep."

We walked a couple more blocks in silence. Then she stopped and turned to me. "Can I tell you something? While we walk?"

"Sure." Here it was. Was I about to hear a sordid confession?

She started walking again. "Self-discipline has always been one of my strong points. When you start to fall apart," she said, "the first thing that goes is your self-discipline. When *that* starts to crack, you know the whole foundation is gradually slipping into the sea. Your moral strength and character, I mean. You take a little away from the whole universe."

"Oh. The universe."

"Yes. Now I'll tell you a story. Which is actually an incident. About, oh, ten weeks ago, I was staying at this hotel in Dallas with Team Donsprokken."

"Dallas again, huh?" I said. "You seem to spend a lot of time in Dallas."

She ignored this. "We were there for a tournament,

staying at a really grand hotel. I was sharing a room with Wendy Call. A good person to share a room with. Sound sleeper, sleeps *late*, you forget she's even there. Except she borrows sweaters without asking. But this hotel, it has a waterfall and a little pond and footbridge *in the lobby*. Can you imagine?"

"I can try."

"Well, after dinner I was walking through the lobby, wearing a yellow-and-blue sundress, with sandals and no socks, and I came to the pond and waterfall and decided I'd be Miss Free Spirit, so I went over to the pond and slipped off my sandals and dangled my feet in. Nobody seemed to mind, the hotel management sort of looked the other way. I'm sitting there dangling my feet in and guess what—the fish, all these fish—I didn't mention there were fish—but they came right up and nibbled at my toes. Honestly. I didn't know fish *did* that. Have you ever had fish nibble at your toes?"

"No," I said. "I had an Uncle Darrell who nibbled at people's toes, though."

"Oh, by the way," she said, "I have to tell you this before I forget. This has nothing to do with anything, but guess who I ran into at poolside at that very same hotel. Take a guess."

"Somebody famous?"

"Yeah, a celebrity. Guess. We'll play Twenty Questions."

How many long walks and boring car trips had we whiled away playing that game?

I needed only sixteen questions to nail it down to a female non-Caucasian singing widow. From there it was easy.

"Yoko? You saw Yoko Ono at poolside?"

Ginny nodded. "We actually had a nice chat."

"What about?"

"Skiing. Snow conditions in Utah. Chair lifts."

"Huh."

"Good job on the Twenty Questions. Anyway, where was I? I was going to tell you about . . . Oh, let's see, it was when I first really noticed I was falling apart. It's an example of my frittering away of self-discipline."

"I'm still trying to figure out what Yoko and the fish and Wendy Call have to do with any of it."

"Well, listen. One morning I woke up at the usual time. Very early. Wendy Call was sound asleep. Nice view of the park outside. Lots of lush green. Usually the first thing I do when I get up is write in my journal. Record my dreams. I don't even get out of bed, just grab my pen and start writing."

"You're not going to tell me about your dreams."

"No, no. Just my routine. Wake up, record dreams. Slide out of bed. Go to bathroom. Splash cold water on face. Break out of dream state."

"You can stop with the Pidgin English," I said. "I'm fairly fluent in the language."

"Sorry. Well, that particular morning in Dallas I rolled over in bed and slept in an extra forty minutes. Not only that, when I did get up, I didn't 'feel' like recording my dreams *and* I couldn't even bring myself to splash cold water on my face. I didn't want the 'discomfort' of the cold water hitting my face. I looked at myself in the mirror and said, 'Why, you lazy old bum.' And that, maybe, was the beginning of my downfall. You reap what you sow."

I nodded. "Ginny, it's stories like that that make people worry about you."

"Oh?"

"It's something you'd hear from some guy wearing a watch cap and ranting and raving in the downtown McDonald's."

"Really?"

"I don't see what it has to do with your coming home or wanting me as your coach."

The shadows were long and the sun was dipping. The breeze carried the smell of woodsmoke and pine and turf. I wanted to tell Ginny that I had missed her, that I had thought about her a lot, that I was glad she was here and hoped she'd stay for a while. We could talk about other things, too. I wanted to tell her about something I had discovered last summer and had been saving for the right person: the Whistling Toilets. I would watch her face when I told her. I didn't think she'd laugh or get repulsed. Then I'd take her there and show her.

There would be time for that, I hoped. Not much time, but some. The question was, would there be a *right* time?

Finally, I simply said, "Ginny, while you're in town, I want you to let me know what I can do for you. Will you do that?"

"Yes. That's nice of you, Stan. Let's walk."

"All right."

" 'Peacock,' " she said. "That's a pretty word, don't you think? I like the sound of that word."

"Peacock," I said. It wasn't a bad-sounding word.

"Let's just keep walking," she said. "Walk beside me. That's what you can do for me."

7

MY PARENTS WERE DELIGHTED to see Ginny. My mother opened one of the cans of fruit cocktail she always kept chilled in the refrigerator for special occasions and sat Ginny at the kitchen table. My father came in from the family room with his June issue of *Digitizer's Digest* and sat down next to Ginny and continued reading it.

I went up to my room to change my socks, which had gotten wet in the gully while I was fishing out golf balls, and to put my new NFL lunch pail in a place where my mother wouldn't grab it and throw it in the trash. I looked at my Lumberjack Luke clock, to see what time it was. Lumberjack Luke's face stared back at me. He was a mean-looking guy to have on the face of your clock. He was not really a lumberjack but a professional big-time wrestler who had wrestled such greats as Ironman, Gunnar Savage, Big Chief Running Bear, and Abdullah the Butcher. Guballa and Wilcutts had found it at a thrift shop and given it to me last Christmas. As a gag, of course. I usually kept it on my hero shelf, next to my stolen copy of *Advantage Ashe*.

Guballa and Wilcutts would be here any minute.

Coming down from my room, I stopped at the foot of the stairs to eavesdrop on the conversation in the kitchen. I was shocked and humiliated. They were talking about me. Me—intimate details of my life, my eating habits, sleeping habits, bowel movements. Good God. But wait a minute. Whoops. Mistake. They weren't talking about me after all but about Ginny's cat, Boat. Relieved, I continued on into the kitchen.

"When are your two chums supposed to be here?" Mom asked.

"Any minute."

"Did you tell them about the honking in the driveway?"

"I told them."

"You told them I said it's got to stop? This business of pulling up in the driveway and blasting their horn because they're too lazy to get out of the car and—"

She was interrupted by a series of honks from the driveway. One long, two short, one long, three short. That was Guballa's signature honk. Wilcutts's signature honk was two, one, three, one. That was so I could tell who was driving. For whatever good that did.

I stood up quickly. "That's them."

"Stan, I thought you said you—"

"I told them, Mom. They must have forgotten."

"Well, maybe I should tell them," Mom said.

More honks.

"Gotta go," I said. "Ginny, I'll give you a call tomorrow."

"Say hi for me," Ginny said.

"Come on out and say it yourself. They'd love to see you."

Ginny's cheeks flushed. "Really? You think they'd . . . ?"

"Sure. They've missed you, too." That *too*—how had that slipped in there? Had she noticed it?

"Stan, honestly," my mother said in a tone I recognized and dreaded. "You boys really need to learn some manners. You are not going to drag Ginny out to the driveway. You are going to invite your friends into the kitchen for five short minutes of civility."

"I don't know if they'll come," I said.

"What do you mean you don't know if they'll come? You're not asking them to the prom. Why wouldn't they come inside the house? You simply invite them in for some fruit cocktail."

My dad finally looked up from his magazine, frowning. He cleared his throat. "Now, Jan. It might be better for your blood pressure if they—"

"My blood pressure is fine, Bill."

Ginny rose. "I really don't mind going out and—"

"Ginny, sit. Stan, go out and tell—invite your two friends in for five little minutes."

My dad let out a long sigh and returned to his reading.

I got up and went out on the front porch. Mom followed me. I signaled Guballa and Wilcutts to come in. I signaled again. They just stared back without expression. They reminded me of a couple of psychiatrists observing a mental patient through a one-way mirror. Blank faces.

Mom was still for a few seconds, watching them. She leaned toward me, not taking her eyes off them. "Are they brain dead or what?"

"They're just not used to this," I said. "Go back in the house, Mom. You're spooking them."

"Oh my God," Mom said.

As soon as my mother had gone back into the house, Wilcutts, on the passenger side, rolled down his window and stuck his head out. "What are you waiting for?"

Next to him, Guballa's hands gripped the steering wheel. His face was a beige smudge.

"Come in for a minute," I said.

My two friends looked at each other as if I had just asked them to come in and try on panty hose.

Wilcutts stuck his head out again. "What for?"

"I've got a mystery guest in the kitchen."

They looked at each other. Then they opened their doors and dragged themselves out of Guballa's Ford LTD.

"Mystery guest," Guballa muttered, digging into his front pocket for his collapsible hairbrush. Wilcutts, who did not carry a collapsible hairbrush, headed for the guest bathroom off the entry way. Guballa checked himself in the hallway mirror, then proceeded to the kitchen, twirling his car keys around his finger.

"Well, well, well," he said when he saw the mystery guest. "If it ain't Martina Notverylovely."

Ginny was blushing. My mom stood over by the sink, hands on her hips. "Dan, you're going to have to knock off the honking. The neighbors don't appreciate it and I—"

"Say no more, Mrs. C.," Guballa said, holding up his hands. "I read you loud and clear. Aw, now, don't be mad." He winked at my father and said huskily, "Us mens are always making these womens mad at us, eh, Bill?"

My dad laughed politely.

My mother's voice was curt, the way it was the morning after she and my dad had had a fight. "Would you like some fruit cocktail?"

"No, thanks, Mrs. Claxton, but I could use something to drink, if you don't mind. None of that diet stuff, please." He gave Ginny a wink. "I'm a natural man."

There was the sound of a toilet flushing, followed

by Wilcutts entering the room zipping his fly. He looked up, his mouth forming an o. "Well, well, well," he said. He still had a tan from spring vacation in Hawaii with his family. "The angels must be having an exchange program, and look who they sent."

"Oh my God," my mother muttered to the ceiling. Then: "Eugene, would you like some fruit cocktail or something to drink?"

"Something to drink's fine, thanks," he said.

"Win any tournaments lately?" he asked Ginny.

"Not lately." Ginny's voice sounded small and unnatural.

"You've parted your hair differently," Wilcutts said. "Looks great."

"Thanks."

"How long you in town for?" he asked.

"I'm not really sure. There's this tournament next week. After that—" She shrugged. "How about you guys? What are you two doing this summer?"

Guballa accepted his drink from my mother, who also handed one to Wilcutts. "We have a tree-pruning business," Guballa said. "We're partners. I do the man's work, he does the ladies'."

"I have all the contacts," Wilcutts said. "I scrape up the customers. Ladies from my church and from my parents' clubs and organizations. *He* does most of the grunt work, but I hold everything together with customer service."

"What did I tell you," Guballa said. "He sips tea

with the old biddies. That's women's work. Women and fags."

"Dan—"

Guballa winced. "Sorry, Mrs. C. I forgot I was in a politically correct zone."

"Drink fast," I said.

Guballa raised his glass. "To all my illegitimate children, wherever they may be." He drank hard, gulped noisily.

My dad chuckled, shaking his head.

"Maybe Ginny would like to come with us," Wilcutts said in his customer-service voice. "Come with us, Ginny. We'll let you ride shotgun."

"Yeah," Guballa said, "come with us."

Ginny thanked them but said she was going to dinner at the club with her parents.

"Got yourself a guy yet?" Guballa asked.

Ginny blushed and said no.

"I don't suppose you'd have much time for that sort of thing," Guballa said. "Besides, most of them tennis geeks are queers anyway." He glanced at my mother. "Sorry, I can't remember whether 'geek' is acceptable or not."

My mother stared at him. "Excuse me? Did I just hear you say that most male tennis players are gay?"

"Well, you have to admit," Guballa said, "it's a pretty faggy game. Most of the gals have hairier legs than the dudes."

"Jan," my father said, "blood pressure. You know Dan's just trying to push your buttons."

"Hey, no, really," Guballa said. "What else do you call a guy who minces around in tight white shorts saying 'love love, deuth deuth.' "

"Time to go," I said. "Hey, guys, let's get going."

I hated playing straight man to these two jokers. Times like this, I was not myself around these two any more than Ginny was *her* self around them. For a moment, I wondered why Ginny and I didn't take off together and spend the evening being ourselves and leave these four here in the kitchen to push each other's buttons.

"While we're on the subject of genders and sports," Guballa said, "what really irks me is when—"

"We're not on the subject, Guballa," I said. "We don't want to hear it."

"Oh, but we do," Mom said, her eyes wide. "Tell us, Dan. I insist. What irks you?"

"It's when they force you to have girls on your team. When I was twelve—"

I groaned. "No, no, Guballa, not this story."

"Stan," my mother said. "Go ahead, Dan. When you were twelve . . ."

"We were forced to have six girls on our soccer team. Their mothers came and made our coach take these six girls. So of course, all of a sudden we have to start not caring about winning. *Wanting* to win is *bad*. Just go out and do your best. Have *fun*. Winning is secondary. Yeah, we had fun all right. Ended up with the worst record in the whole league. Those girls. They couldn't tackle, couldn't dribble, couldn't pass, couldn't shoot, couldn't stay in position. One or the other of 'em was always rushing off in tears. The only time they didn't cry was when we lost. *Then* they were the most cheerful bunch you'd ever want to see, they couldn't wait to line up and exchange high fives with the winning team. It makes me shudder just thinking about it. It left a scar on me. Really, it left a scar."

I managed to get Guballa out of the house before my mother left scars of her own. We stopped at a drive-thru and ordered hamburgers and ate them while we were cruising around.

Wilcutts said, "Well, Guballa, you dazzled them again. Your usual brazen obnoxious performance."

"Little Ginny," Guballa said. He was doing thirty in the right-hand lane where the speed limit was forty. "Did you see those slender, sinewy arms?" Guballa was an arm man. "What a tootsie," he said. "Is she a tootsie or what? And she gets prettier every year. She's one of those rare girls who has beauty *in* her, not just *on* her."

"How poetic," Wilcutts said. "Where'd you steal that from?"

Guballa looked at me in the rearview mirror. "Stan, same question I asked you the other day. Maybe you don't want to call it the hots, but where do you stand with Ginny? Where do you *want* to stand with Ginny? Where do you see you two going?"

"I haven't thought about it," I said.

"I'll give you fifteen minutes," Guballa said.

He swung a right turn up 125th, heading west, toward Puget Sound.

"She really does have a quality," Wilcutts said, folding his arms. "An *inner* quality, you know?"

"Didn't I just say that, you idiot?" Guballa said.

"She's the kind of girl," Wilcutts said dreamily, "you'd go to the *zoo* with. Or to a Shakespeare festival, or the post office, or feed the ducks, or—"

"Yeah, we get the point!" Guballa snapped. "It ain't that profound. Gee, you mean there's some girls you'd like to do more than get in their pants? Wow!"

I did not like where this was heading. I didn't want to hear them talking about pants and Ginny in this old Ford LTD, where so many lewd conversations had taken place.

Guballa, as if he sensed what I was thinking, said, "Claxton, I'll be honest with you. This is no bull. I think I felt something between Ginny and me in the kitchen. Something real."

"Oh God!" Wilcutts broke into laughter. "Oh, Guballa, that's precious!"

"Pardon me, can I get a little respect for sharing my feelings?" Guballa said. This only made Wilcutts laugh harder, tears springing from his eyes, his throat gagging. Guballa's hands tightened on the steering wheel. "At the risk of being crass and vulgar, Stan, I guess I need to spell it out for you. It's your call; you can stake a claim on Ginny or not stake a claim on Ginny. You have dibs. If you relinquish your dibs, then . . ."

"Then what?" Wilcutts said, wiping his tears.

"Then I'll ask the little darlin' out myself."

"She wouldn't go out with you," Wilcutts snorted.

"That's never stopped me before. I'll tell you this much, Wilcutts, she'd go out with me before she went out with you."

"That," Wilcutts said, popping two Rolaids into his mouth, "is extremely debatable. Need I remind anyone that my lips"—he pursed them and pointed to them—"these lips, are the only ones in this car that have actually touched Ginny."

"I wouldn't brag about that if I were you," Guballa said.

"I wouldn't either," I put in.

"I'm not," Wilcutts said. "I'm not bragging."

"Then why did you bring it up?" I said.

"Because," Wilcutts said. "Because I still think about it, that's why."

"Listen," Guballa said, "if Claxton would just stake his claim on her, it would simplify things for all of us. We'd step back and throw all our support behind him."

"Guballa," I said, shaking my head.

Guballa pulled over to the curb and the three of

us got out. We walked down some cement stairs to a
bench, where we could sit and watch the postcard
view of Puget Sound and the Olympic Mountains.
This was one of our favorite lookouts. The sun had set
over an hour ago, but the sky was still light and changing colors. We sat on the bench, a respectable distance
from one another's personal space, and I hoped,
hoped they would not mention Ginny again.

"Will you look at that," Guballa said.

"Doodle doodle damn," Wilcutts said.

The sky, streaked with clouds, filled me with a deep
untouchable longing. I thought of the Whistling Toilets. I had to say something, no matter how dumb it
sounded. I said, "Love is untouchable. It's spirit. You
can't—you don't stake a claim on it. You don't call
dibs. Love is—it's like that sky—it's a—it's a contin-
uous unfolding."

"So is getting laid," Wilcutts said.

We watched the horizon, each thinking his own
thoughts.

"Look at that sky, those clouds," Guballa said.

Salmon, pink, orange, purple, red. Radiant, wispy
clouds. Blue solid mountains.

Guballa didn't look at me, but placed his hand on
my shoulder. His face glowed from the western sky.

8

"HOW WAS YOUR NIGHT OUT with Guballa
and Wilcutts?"

It was two days later, Sunday afternoon. I hadn't
seen Ginny on Saturday; she'd had errands and I'd
gone over things with the sub. His name was Jeff
Grange; he was a freshman P.E. major at the Univer-
sity of Washington and he wanted to do this for only
a couple of weeks and wasn't too thrilled about it, but
he was getting credits toward his major. Maggie had
okayed him, but she was still looking for a permanent
replacement and wasn't having much luck. Grange
would be taking over Tuesday. On Monday I'd present
him to the runts and let him observe my Vince Lombardi coaching technique. "Your who coaching technique?" he'd asked. Vince Lombardi, I had said,
glaring at him. He had stared back with a dorky grin.

"What, you gonna wear a glittery sequin tuxedo and foof your hair and play the piano for them?" It took me a minute to realize he was talking about Liberace. The Liberace coaching technique. I didn't bother correcting him.

He had, however, heard of my tennis racket, and he asked me where I'd gotten it. I gave him the same answer I gave everybody who asked about it: Rich uncle in England sent it to me.

"Do you think I could borrow it while you're—"

"No."

So now, Sunday afternoon, Ginny and I were out walking, catching up.

"My night with those two was no stranger than usual," I said. "You were the main topic of conversation."

"Really? I don't know if I want to hear about that."

"Maybe not."

We walked on down the street. She looked at me. "Why wouldn't I want to hear about it? Was it bad?"

"What's it matter to you? Unless of course you *care* about what they think of you."

"Ha."

"You can tell me if you care," I said. "And don't worry; it was all good. They had only good things to say about you."

"Like what?"

"You *do* want to hear about it."

"A morsel or two, maybe."

"A morsel or two. Well, they said you have a quality. An inner quality. That you're pretty, but the pretty isn't just on you, it's in you."

"They said that?"

"Yes."

"So I'm plain on the outside or something?"

"And your eyes," I said, "your eyes light up when you do such and such. And when you laugh, you crinkle your nose and all the birds tweet a little louder."

"Oh bull. You're teasing."

"Paraphrasing a bit, but they said most of it."

"That Dan Guballa," she said, shaking her head. "What a cocky, arrogant, smug . . . *traumatized* when he was twelve. I know a few girls who could traumatize him now—run him right into the ground on a soccer field. *And* they shave their legs. He's living in the Dark Ages and he doesn't even know it."

"Why didn't you speak up the other night?"

She sighed. "Because. You know. I get inhibited. I can't even swallow when I'm around those two jerks, for some reason."

"Sounds like a crush," I said, keeping my voice light but feeling something strange and uncomfortable creeping through me.

Ginny didn't say anything, which meant she didn't deny it. We walked past a small shop that used to be a grocery store. It had gone out of business three years ago and was now a dog-grooming parlor.

"The old Chinaman place," Ginny said. "I can't believe we all called it that. We knew better."

"Your dad and my dad called it that when they were kids," I said.

"Walking into that place was an experience," Ginny said. "All that candy, covered with a fine layer of dust. After school, he'd only let in three kids at a time. We had to line up outside on the sidewalk. How degrading."

"Whenever I walk by this place," I said, "I burp Hostess cherry pies."

"Oh God, Hostess pies," she said, laughing. "I'd forgotten that. It makes me queasy just thinking about it. We sure got on some strange food kicks."

"We got on some good food kicks, too," I said.

"Yeah, we did," she said. She gave it some thought. "Like what, for instance?"

"I don't know. Give me a minute."

We walked on past two or three other shops.

"I suppose I'd have to admit Guballa's kind of *interesting*," Ginny said. "I think he tries to be a redneck, but he's really not one. He's deeper than he lets on. And he's romantic. I wouldn't call it a crush, though."

"How about Wilcutts?" I asked.

"Oh, he's interesting, too. In a more tame and civilized way than Guballa. They're both very gentlemanly, you know. Old-fashioned."

"Old-fashioned. Glazed old-fashioned doughnuts and chocolate milk," I said.

"What?"

"That was one of our good food kicks. And malted-milk balls and pepperoni sticks. And cashews."

"Ah, cashews," Ginny said. "Good old Chinaman place."

"He was a mean old Chinaman," I said.

"He was good to his family, though," Ginny said. "I used to envy all his children and grandchildren and nieces and nephews. They all worked and played around the store. They were always there. I'm sure they had their own problems, but they seemed . . . harmonious."

Later on, Ginny and I practiced for two hours at a nearby tennis court. It felt like the old days. Also, as I'd done many times before, I brought a push broom to sweep away the twigs and dirt, while she tightened the net. It was good hitting with her on that court we had spent so many hours of our lives on, working up a sweat, doing the drills and patterns that Donsprokken had outlined in the notebook he'd given me. Afterward, cooling off, we took the path down to the creek and sat on the footbridge. It had no railings, so we could sit on the edge of it and dangle our feet inches above the shallow water flowing by. Ginny had brought a plastic bread sack full of chocolate-chip cupcakes that she'd made Saturday night, and a thermos of cold lemonade. The cake was gooey and the chips were hard. They were good cupcakes.

"Did you really make these?" I asked with my mouth full.

"Yeah, you want another?"

"When I'm done with this one."

"You know," Ginny said, looking down at her tennis shoes, "there's something that's been bothering me. About Wilcutts."

"Wilcutts? What's been bothering you about Wilcutts?"

"Well, I was trying to remember . . . it's really been bugging me. Didn't Wilcutts try to kiss me in the fourth grade?"

"Try? He *did* kiss you."

"No, he didn't."

"Yes, he did."

"No, he tried, but—"

"He succeeded, Ginn. I guarantee it. I was there. I remember every detail. He remembers it, too."

"Wilcutts does?"

"Yeah. He brings it up all the time. He brought it up Friday night. It still bugs him."

"Oh, come on."

"Really. He tends to obsess about things. He doesn't pop Rolaids all the time for nothing, you know."

"But why . . . why would he be *bothered* by it six years later? Was it that bad for him?"

"Terrible. Must not've been too great for you, either, since you seem to have blocked it right out of your memory. Of course, I wouldn't blame you if you had. If Wilcutts kissed me, I'd block it out, too. Plus the fact that eleven guys were holding you down."

"Oh, I remember that part! It really took eleven?"

"Give or take a couple now and then."

"How lurid," she said. "Maybe I really have blocked it out. I sure don't remember Wilcutts actually completing the kiss. I remember the situation. The playground. Recess, right?"

"Lunchtime. Noon recess."

"Out on the playfield?"

"The very same one you were whacking golf balls on the other day."

"Were you one of the eleven? Holding me down?"

"No. I was helping Wilcutts get his courage up."

"Aha. You were a coach even back then. But . . . you're sure he actually got it up? His courage, I mean. You haven't embroidered it over the years?"

"Ginny, I see it like it was yesterday. You know, those eleven guys, they didn't actually hold you on the ground. They held you upright."

"Vertical."

"Yes. They served franks and beans for lunch that day."

"Who did?"

"The cafeteria. I'm just showing you how clearly I remember that day. Every detail. I remember the length and color of your hair. You wore one of those plastic semicircles—what do you call those?"

"Headbands?"

"Yeah. And you were wearing denim coolants."

"That's not what they're called, but I know what you mean. Wow, Stan, I'm impressed."

"You sat at the fourth-graders' table, naturally. We fifth-graders all taunted Wilcutts during lunch. Egged him on. We knew he liked you. We dared him to kiss you. Back then, it was easy to make Wilcutts laugh while he was drinking his milk. You just waited for him to start drinking, then you made funny faces and he'd crack up and lose control and snort his milk out through his nose. We called it Wilcutts Falls. We did it to him that day, got him to gush his milk out through his nose. Well, maybe that gave him the courage he needed. He threw down the gauntlet, you might say. He vowed he would kiss you whether you wanted it or not."

"I should be the one traumatized, not him."

"No question. But I really don't think you minded it all that much at the time. While they were chasing you, you had a sort of panicked-doe look on your face, but you didn't seem to be minding it that much."

"I suppose it's flattering when somebody goes to such great lengths to kiss you. All that attention."

"Attention? You'd been on center court in plenty of big matches by then. You'd been written up in the papers. You'd gotten plenty of spotlight."

"Yeah, but you can't compare *that* to being held down by eleven guys and kissed by someone who's just been snorting milk out his nose."

"I suppose not."

"Did he kiss me on the lips?" Ginny asked.

"Ah, you've asked the key question. Now picture it. There you are, being held like a caught animal, and I'm there spurring Wilcutts on. He finally goes and gives you a kiss right here. Right here."

Wiping the crumbs off my right index finger, I tapped the bridge of Ginny's nose, where six years ago Wilcutts had put his lips.

"Here? On my nose?"

"Yes. The bridge."

"Why? Was his aim that bad?"

"No, he was on target. And that's what's haunted him ever since. He's worried he has some kinky nose-bridge fetish."

"Why did he do it there? Did he say why?"

"Yes. Yes, he did."

She waited a moment. "Are you going to tell me?"

"Maybe you don't want to hear it," I said.

"Oh, not this again. We already went through this. Why wouldn't I want to hear it?"

"Well now, suppose Wilcutts were to ask you out. You might—you might—" I stopped. Something almost imperceptible had come into her face.

She glanced up at me. "He did."

"Did what? Ask you out?"

"Last night. Called me."

"What time?"

"Seven-ten. On the nose—no pun intended."

"Seven-ten," I said. "He's probably read that 7:10 is the ideal time to call a girl. He's got this book of dating do's and don'ts, I think it's his great-grandfather's Boy Scout manual from 1937 or something. Somewhere in his brain he's got the idea that the perfect time for calling a girl is 7:10."

"Well," Ginny said, "it *was* a pretty good time. I was cleaning the frosting off the Mixmaster General. You can't do anything while cleaning the Mixmaster General except talk on the phone."

"What'd he say? Was he nervous?"

"Not really. More businesslike. He got right to the point."

"What did *you* say?"

"I told him I wasn't going to think about doing anything until after this tournament."

"So, you implied you might think about doing something *after* the tournament?"

"I don't know what I implied. I don't care. I'm not going to let anything distract me. Besides, I think it was all a big joke. Five minutes after I hung up, Guballa called."

"Guballa, too, eh?"

"Yeah. I hadn't even finished cleaning the Mixmas-

ter General. I figured they were either playing a joke
or having some dumb guy-contest. So I said the same
thing to Guballa that I said to Wilcutts."

"Wait a minute," I said. "Doesn't Nancy clean the
Mixmaster General? Isn't that her job?"

"She has a public-speaking class Saturday eve-
nings."

"Aha," I said. "You mean she was doing Toastmas-
ter when she should have been doing Mixmaster." I
couldn't resist.

Ginny rolled her eyes. "Why don't you go ahead
and tell me."

"Tell you what?"

"What on earth was his reason for kissing me on
my nose?"

"Oh. The freckles."

"Huh?"

"It was the freckles. According to Wilcutts, he was
both attracted to and repelled by the freckles on the
bridge of your nose. He wanted to see if they had any
taste or feel."

"He told you that?"

"Yes."

"The freckles on my . . ." She reached up and felt
them with her fingers. "Did they? What did they feel
like?"

"Cold and hard."

"I should hope so," Ginny said.

9

ON MONDAY Jeff Grange met me at Sour Lake, and I introduced him to the runts and told them he'd be filling in for me for a few days while I was on a Secret Mission for the CIA. I didn't tell them I was leaving for good. I couldn't. Grange sat at courtside taking notes while I put the runts through their paces for the last time. One last time. Ginny had ridden her bike over and was watching. I introduced her to the runts as someone who would one day be a professional tennis player and play at Wimbledon and the U.S. Open. The runts were suitably impressed, but not as impressed as my going on a Secret Mission for the CIA.

I decided to leave Jeff Grange on his own for the final half hour of practice. I said goodbye to the kids, feeling a curious tightening in my throat. I assured them they were in good hands with Jeff.

As Ginny and I were leaving, Grange came running after me. "Hey, Stan, about your tennis racket. Suppose I were to borrow it just for a—"

"No."

I wished him luck. I waved to my team.

Ginny and I rode our bikes side by side down the street. She said, "You know, I have to admit, you really are pretty good with those kids."

"I'm a glorified babysitter, is what I am."

"You make it fun for them. I know you know that. You've always been good at enjoying things, making things fun for people. That's a gift."

"Yeah," I said, "it's called being a professional clown."

She laughed. "A clown babysitter. There must be a big demand for that. But you know, when you were saying goodbye to them, I felt myself get a little choked up. Like you really *were* going on a dangerous mission."

"Well," I said, hesitating for a second, "I think it was a permanent goodbye."

"What?"

I told her about Donsprokken's offer, watching her reaction. She didn't seem to have much of one, although she said it was a great opportunity and all that. But her eyes didn't quite reflect the words. Why not? Maybe she didn't want me to go.

"It *is* a pretty good opportunity," I said. She agreed. Then I said, "I don't know if I'd call it a *gift*. But there is a sort of knack to it, making it fun. The idea of having fun at something just for the heck of it."

She smiled. "And not caring about winning or being great? Oh boy, don't let Guballa hear you say that. But I know what you mean. It *is* a gift."

"Maybe."

"I've gotten it before," Ginny said. "I used to get it a lot. You feel blessed, just because you're in a close match against a good opponent and you're having to scrape for every point and really work."

"You don't get it anymore?"

"Not lately. Well, you know, I'm getting old—fifteen. You should see some of those ten- and eleven-year-olds coming up through the ranks, Stan. It's scary, I mean it. I'm scared to death."

"Of what? Besides ten- and eleven-year-olds."

"Of doing the wrong thing. Not being good enough. Letting my parents and Donsprokken down. Letting *myself* down. Being selfish and self-centered. Missing out on life. Or missing out on tennis."

"Have you ever thought of giving up tennis?" I asked. "At least giving up the fast track. Just coming home and playing at the club and going to high school. Would it be that bad?"

"Bad? I don't know. Is it bad to give up something you've worked your whole life for? Isn't that a waste?

I don't know. I've thought about it, yes. But I can't
see myself playing on the school team."

"You'd be number one."

"Gosh, how thrilling. You mean I'd *letter*? And
what about you? You could make the team. You could
play tennis for the glory of your school. But you're not
a *team* player, are you."

She knew my history in this area, my one horrible
experience with team sports. I had told her the story
many times. It had happened, strangely enough, on
the seventh-grade football team. I was a lean and wiry
halfback, jersey number 22. The incident changed my
life. Or at least changed my attitude about team sports
once and for all.

It was a boiling hot afternoon in late September.
At halftime we had come in out of the heat to sit on
the cool floor of the breezeway, while our coach be-
rated us because we were behind 12–0. A wet towel
was being passed from player to player, so that each
player could wipe his sweaty face with it. This struck
me as extremely gross. And yet, when I was handed
the cool, wet towel, I went ahead and mopped my
sweaty face with it, just like everybody else.

Then I handed it to Walter Waggoner, our meaty
left guard, who had a face like a hog. When he took
the towel, he did not wipe his face with it; he put his
big lips to the towel and started sucking the water
from it. He sat there sucking and sucking. I watched
in horror. I couldn't tear my eyes away.

I finished out the season, but it was the one and only team I ever played on.

Tuesday morning, the tournament draw was to be posted. Bitsy invited me over for breakfast. Dirk had gone downtown on business. Nancy had set up a help-yourself buffet in the parlor. At 8:05 Bitsy telephoned the club that was hosting the tournament, to find out who Ginny was playing in the first round and what time the match was scheduled for.

By 8:07 Bitsy was shouting into the phone. "That's crazy! Don't give me that. Let me talk to the head official. What are you trying to pull? My daughter is a nationally ranked player. She's doing you a favor by even showing up in your little tournament."

Ginny and I sat on the couch with our plates before us on the coffee table. Ginny was wearing shorts but had a blanket over her legs. She stopped chewing her coffee cake. "Since when do you put catsup on your scrambled eggs?"

I shrugged. "When was the last time you saw me *not* put catsup on my scrambled eggs?"

Bitsy hung up. "Well, isn't that just yummy. I don't believe it. I'm going to call Donsprokken. We might have to tell them to take their no-brain tournament and shove it."

She explained. There were only thirty-two slots in the eighteen-and-under singles category, which was what Ginny had entered. But forty-six girls had en-

tered it, so some of the girls had to play qualifying
matches; the winners would advance to the group of
thirty-two. Of course, the established players, the well-
known players, the nationally ranked players, would
never have to bother with qualifying matches. It was
the no-names, the struggling unknowns, the last-
minute entries who had to earn their way into a tournament slot. Ginny wasn't one of those, but they were
making her play a qualifying match anyway. The
match was scheduled for tomorrow at 10:30 a.m.

"It is an absolute, intentional slap in the face to
you, to me, to your father, to your sponsors, and to
Donsprokken." Bitsy glanced at me. Apparently my
face was unslapped. "I think the people at that club
have got a grudge against Donsprokken. They're mad
because he bypasses their tournament every year. But,
good grief, it's second-rate, don't they know that?
They don't even use *linesmen* until the third round.
Ginny, you know how hard it is for me to watch you
play a match when you have to call your own lines. I
end up biting my nails and getting dizzy and my throat
gets sore for the next two—"

"Mom, it's okay. We already agreed you and Dad
won't come and watch me until the third round. Stan'll
be with me. You two make me more nervous than you
make yourselves."

The phone rang. Bitsy grabbed it. "Yes. Yes, thank
you. I would like to know who my daughter, Ginny

Forrester, is scheduled to play in her—in her *quali-fying round*." Bitsy waited, her eyes flicking about the room. "Who? Who the hell is that? Who's her father? Which club?"

Ginny turned to me. "I saw you eat scrambled eggs two years ago at your house. You didn't put catsup on them then."

"That's because I was having them for dinner that time. I don't put catsup on them when I'm having them for dinner. Only for breakfast."

"Doesn't it make the eggs cold? I hate it when—" She stopped and looked at Bitsy, who had just hung up.

"Well!" Bitsy said, shaking her head. "I've never heard of her. Nobody's ever heard of her."

"What's her name?" Ginny asked.

"She belongs to a very exclusive club in Woodin-ville. Daughter of a big shot. Seems we're talking megabucks here. She's probably had private lessons since she was a toddler. *Why* has no one ever heard of her? I'm going to call Donsprokken."

"Mother. Her name."

"Oh. Didn't I tell you? Antonia Wheeler."

Ginny repeated the name. "I've never heard of her."

"I *know* that, sweetie, no one has. She's an *un-known*. Maybe Donsprokken's heard of her. I'm going to make some phone calls and see what I can dig up about this Wheeler girl. I don't see how she could be anything to worry about, but I don't like unknowns. Nancy! Are you out there? Would you please get me my address book from on top of my dressing table? Kids, I'm going to sit here and be on the phone all morning. Why don't you two leave me alone and I'll let you know what I find out."

We took our plates out to the kitchen and helped Nancy clean up. Then we packed a picnic lunch and took off on a bike ride. We rode along the Burke-Gilman trail, a paved path that was nice and flat. Most of the ride, we didn't say much, just enjoyed the scenery. We stopped at a park and ate our peanut butter-and-jelly sandwiches and didn't talk much then, either. On we rode. Ginny seemed preoccupied, probably starting to worry about her match tomorrow.

"Stan," she said, "there's something I've been meaning to tell you."

Uh-oh. I didn't like the sound of that. Maybe there was more on her mind than tomorrow's match. Was this going to be her big confession? All about the tennis twerp she'd fallen for? I didn't want to hear about it. We were having a good ride, why spoil it? But if she had to get it off her chest before her match tomorrow, then I'd have to shut up and listen.

"What's that?" I asked.

"Well, I've heard this voice in my head. It says the same thing. It says— Wait a minute, let's get off our bikes for a while."

"It tells you to get off your bike?"

"No, no, I'll tell you in a second."

We got off our bikes and sat down on a bench.

"So," I said. "A voice has spoken to you."

"Yes. On two—no, three occasions since I've been home. It spoke to me about twenty minutes ago."

"Is this a heavenly voice?"

"I don't see why not. Now don't smirk."

"Is it a he or a she?"

Ginny thought. "I think it's a she."

"Well, that rules out God or the Voice of Reason."

"Ha ha."

"What does the voice say?"

"It says, 'Let's just fool around until we get caught.' Or 'Let's keep on playing until we get caught.' Some variation of that. Does that mean anything to you?"

"Of course," I said without hesitation. "Don't you remember that? It was when we had that big snow three years ago. School was closed for three days. Except," I said, "those weren't the exact words. The exact words were 'Let's just *play* until we get caught.' "

"Some heavenly voice," Ginny said. "It didn't even get the quote right."

On one of those snow days Ginny and I had walked to the junior high. The air had been clear and cold. The snow had crunched under our boots. We lugged our bags containing our tennis shoes. I was carrying my basketball. Ginny was twelve, I was thirteen. Our mission: to see if the gym was open for basketball. We had heard it might be.

It wasn't. Nobody was there; the place was deserted. But we tried all the doors, and by some miracle, one of the side doors leading into the gym was locked but hadn't been completely shut, so that if you pushed, it opened. A true miracle. Maybe there *was* something heavenly involved.

We had gone into the gym. The lights weren't on, but we didn't need them, the windows were bright white. We had peeled off our outer clothes to our gym clothes underneath. We shot baskets, played Horse, Around the World, Twenty-one. The whole gym was ours, with snow falling dizzily outside. We kept stopping to look around, knowing any minute a custodian or some other authority figure would come along and tell us we weren't supposed to be there and kick us out. So we agreed we'd just play until we got caught.

"It seems like that always happens," Ginny said, pulling up one of her socks. "Whenever you're doing something fun, you always feel like you're on the verge of being interrupted by some 'grownup' telling you you're someplace you're not supposed to be, doing something you're not supposed to be doing. My question is, does that make what you're doing more fun or less fun?"

"More," I said.

"You think so?"

"Sure. A little friction and tension stimulate your senses. It's like that splash of cold water you take every morning." I was listening to myself and wondering if I really believed it. If so, why had I spent so much of my life trying to avoid friction and tension?

"It's like that time we hiked up to Barrow Falls," Ginny said. "That's one of my all-time greatest memories. We hiked all the way up to the falls and ate lunch, just the two of us, no one else around."

"What does that have to do with playing basketball in the gym on that snow day. That's not the same—"

"Well, let me finish. We ate, we hiked back down. Your mom was going to pick us up at five o'clock. We got to the trailhead at ten to five. Perfect timing. Now, during the entire hike up to the falls, we had talked very little, right? And again, during our lunch, no conversation. Loud gushing falls. No talk."

"But—"

"Stan, let me finish. The point is, all day we hadn't talked much, and when we got back to the trailhead at ten to five, waiting for your mom to show up at five, we started a conversation, quite by accident. A great conversation. It turned out to be, in my opinion, one of the best conversations we've ever had. I will never, never forget that conversation. It was momentous. And the whole time, you see, we were wondering where your mom was, she was due to show up any minute, and that would be the end of the conversation. But five minutes went by. Not there yet. Five more minutes. Another five. We said more in that twenty minutes than all the hike up to the falls and back. The same law applies as that snow day in the gym."

"I don't even remember the conversation," I said.

Ginny blinked. "You *don't*?"

"I'm afraid not."

She stared another moment. How many people would have been indignant? Lots. But Ginny burst out laughing.

"It'll come to me in a minute," I said, laughing along with her. "Give me a hint."

"It doesn't matter, anyway," she said. "It's just a memory. It's not real anymore. The minute something becomes the past, it no longer exists."

"Is that what we were talking about at Barrow Falls?"

"What? No, no. But listen. There'll never be another snow day. You wouldn't be able to relive it, even if you could spend millions of dollars reconstructing the exact situation of the gym being open, down to the last detail that day, it would never be the same. It would be artificial. Why? I guess because we're always changing. Those moments—those gifts—they come along and surprise us, they happen by accident. You can't force them or think about them or—or *will* them. That's why they're gifts. Like in tennis, when you're not really expecting it, the gift hits you. No, not *hit*, that's the wrong word. It comes over you, like a mood or like the wind blowing right through you. Or like that song, 'Amazing Grace.' It chooses you. Have you ever felt it, Stan? Has it ever happened to you?"

"Once when I was vacuuming the rug, I sort of became One with the vacuum cleaner."

She gave me a look. "Yeah. Well, hm. Anyway. That's what we were talking about, more or less, that day at Barrow Falls."

Why had I said that about the vacuum cleaner? I could have told her about the Whistling Toilets. But what if I told her and it came out all wrong or she reacted wrong? It would spoil everything. I knew that was a pathetic reason for not telling her. But I had to wait until it felt right. It just didn't feel right.

After our bike ride we had a short tennis workout. Then we split up to shower and have an early dinner. Later, we got together again in Ginny's parlor to watch a video we had checked out from the library, called *High Times in the Big Wahoos*. It was rated PG-13. There was some surfing in it, some snowboarding, rock music, fistfights, boys getting slapped in the face by girls, girl fights, and two instances of fornication. The actors were all unknowns and low-budget. Ginny and I laughed and made wisecracks throughout. Twice she sighed and said, "I wish I didn't have a match tomorrow." And once she mentioned going off to her cabin.

One of the actresses, whose acting was stiff and

wooden as a snowboard, removed her bikini top and showed her bare breasts for what felt like an endless time. Ginny and I didn't look at each other.

After the movie we played Scrabble. The first word Ginny made was "shooter." It struck me as an odd word. Then, smiling, she took the S off the front and stuck it on the end. "Hooters." We looked at each other and laughed.

Bitsy came into the room while we were laughing. "All right. I'll tell you what I've learned about this Antonia Wheeler person. She's seventeen. Her family is— 'Hooters'?" Bitsy frowned at the Scrabble board. "Is that really a word? I'd have challenged that. You could've used 'shooter.' Anyway. Her family's loaded, originally from L.A., now living way out past Wood-inville. They're members of *the* most prestigious club in that area. I telephoned the head pro, Rolly Ber-mann, who has never given the girl a lesson or even seen her play. No one has. I called everybody. Don-sprokken's never heard of her. It's really weird, but I just don't see how she can pose a threat. I don't want you to worry. Stan, don't let Ginny worry."

Ginny and I decided to call off our Scrabble game. It had been a very long day.

"She'll be a knockout," Ginny said, staring at the lone word on the board. "Rich family, tons of class, a name like Antonia. She'll come driving up in a flashy red convertible with her top down. Just like Veronica in *High Times in the Big Wahoos*. With a big old set of hooters."

"Big hooters are a detriment in tennis," I pointed out. "Not only do they get in the way but—"

Ginny rolled her eyes. "Oh, please. How would you even know?"

10

"I DON'T SEE what she's so worried about," Wilcutts said later that night. I had decided to walk over
to Guballa's apartment complex. I was glad to find
them in the cabana, playing eight ball. I needed to
talk.

"She always agonizes before a tournament," I said.
"Especially in the early rounds. It tapers off. The farther she advances, the less nervous she gets before
each match. But this qualifying match has got her even
more worried than usual. She's playing a total un-
known. A mystery."

"She can't expect to have heard of everybody," Wilcutts said.

"You'd be surprised in these local tournaments," I
said. "These girls all know each other, or at least
they've heard of each other. They play in the same

tournaments, belong to one of the handful of clubs. So it's unusual that not a single one of Bitsy's contacts has ever heard of Antonia Wheeler."

"They're afraid she's good or something?"

"That's it," I said. "Odds are, she's a dud. But there's always the slim chance that Antonia Wheeler could be a great player who's been kept a secret. And for whatever reason, now's the time her handlers have decided to bring her out."

We shot pool for a while. I kept talking on and on, wanting them to ask me more questions. Then I realized I hadn't seen them since Ginny had been home.

"All right," I said. "What was the idea calling Ginny up Saturday?"

"Thought you'd never ask," Guballa said. "We did it for you, you know."

"I figured you did," I said. "In some warped way."

"It was like an experiment," Wilcutts said. "A test."

"I don't see what it proved," I said. "Only that she's like every other girl in this city: she doesn't want to go out with either of you two."

"Ouch, that's cruel," Wilcutts said. "But it proves quite a bit. It proves . . . Tell him what it proves, O Guballa."

"It proves," Guballa said, "that she's not just some fifteen-year-old who's looking for a fling. If she was that, she'd have gone out with me and told her tennis to get screwed. On the other hand, if she was in some kind of rebellion against her parents, or some perverted form of self-destruction and self-loathing, then she'd have gone out with Boy Wilcutts over there."

"I get the feeling she's covering something up," I said. "She's involved in something."

"Have you asked her about it?" Guballa said.

I shook my head. "She'll tell me when she's ready."

Guballa's eyes bore into me. "Yeah. In other words, you're afraid to ask her. You're afraid to hear what she's into."

Around ten o'clock the three of us went up to Guballa's apartment, but his brother chased us out because he had a girl there. We went out for hamburgers in Wilcutts's car, but I only got a Coke, because I had made up my mind that before going home I'd walk past Ginny's house and check to make sure she was in bed. She'd probably be awake, worrying. If so, I'd stop in and chew her out for not being in bed. In which case I didn't want hamburger in my stomach or onions on my breath or lettuce between my teeth.

I left the cabana around 11:30 and walked at a leisurely pace. It was a pleasant balmy June night, the bright moon yellow and glowing, dogs yapping, frogs croaking. On such a clear, fragrant, magical night, maybe something would happen. Maybe something had already happened—inside me.

What might my life have been like had I been more ambitious and driven? If I had cared more about achieving some dream? Was the meaning of life to find a dream that you love passionately and pursue it with all your heart? Or was it just to work at being happy and to accept life as it came and accept yourself as you were?

What had I ever cared passionately about in my life?

Tennis? I had been a rising star once. On the fast track, the club circuit. Ginny's mixed-doubles partner. But my interest had gradually faded until, by the time I was thirteen, I enjoyed hitting balls but I had no desire to play tournament tennis. "That doesn't make a bit of sense," people told me. "Hitting balls around isn't tennis. It's just practicing." I still enjoyed going to the summer tennis camps with Ginny, even though I'd been chucked as her doubles partner. I enjoyed working with Rick Donsprokken. I loved watching how he motivated people and drove them and made them go farther than they thought they could go.

Giving up competitive tennis was one of the few things I'd done in my life that I felt had some integrity and honor. It had been a relief not to be such a financial drain on my parents. Donsprokken's fees, the club membership, summer camps, tournament fees—it all added up to a huge expense for my parents. The amount of money they shelled out on my tennis, they could have bought a condo on Maui.

So why, really, had I given it up? Why had I lost interest? I had a tendency to choke under pressure. The more pressure, the worse I played and the less fun it was and the more errors I committed. Volleying into the net, blowing an overhead, double-faulting. Chokes. And yet the funny thing was, my blatant chokes never really bothered me. I didn't stamp or cuss or roll my eyes or shake my head in disgust. I didn't show any remorse at my blown shot. That was the way Arthur Ashe had played, too. He never lost his cool. But with me, people thought I didn't care and wasn't trying hard enough; they thought my heart wasn't in it. Maybe they were right.

But now Donsprokken had offered me something huge: a place where I could work toward a goal. To become an instructor. A teacher. A coach. A pro. Someone who developed young talent, talent that was driven, directed, elite; that would *go* somewhere and *do* something in life. Not a bunch of latchkey runts. That was a noble goal, wasn't it? To be a teacher? I wasn't interested in being a great player but in teaching others how to be, and I had the opportunity to apprentice at one of the best camps in the state. And the romance and cavorting and pairing up among counselors; I could live with that. It was better than my encounters with girls up to now. All right, maybe it wasn't a noble goal in itself, but it was something to look forward to.

The houses on Ginny's street were dark except for their porch lights. What were the odds of her bedroom light being on, with Ginny up there doing something compulsive, worrying about tomorrow, something weird and "busy," like organizing her earring box or washing her sunglasses or juicing grapefruits. When she was younger, the night before a tournament, she'd stay up cutting out pictures of celebrities from Bitsy's magazines. She'd paste them on white plasterboard. It was sickening. Thank God she'd grown out of that.

There was no light on in her bedroom. I was both relieved and disappointed.

Then I noticed a light downstairs. A blue light, not the flicker of a television screen, but the glow of a computer monitor.

I stepped up to the bay window of the parlor. The curtains were parted and one of the windows was open a few inches. Ginny was sitting at the desk in front of the computer, tapping away on the keyboard. When had she learned to type so fast?

Peering in, I felt like a Peeping Tom. You could get shot for this, Claxton.

I tapped on the window, hoping I wouldn't startle her out of her pants. Actually, she wasn't wearing pants but a lavender bathrobe. She didn't jump. Just turned her head and wiggled her fingers in a wave. "Crawl on in," she said.

I crawled in and fell on the carpet with a thud.

She swiveled her chair to face me. Her robe split up to her thighs, revealing smooth pink legs, shiny shins—the left shin had a round bruise on it. There was a freshly bathed look to her, a soapy, lotiony scent. Her hair was in a loose ponytail, tied with a light-blue ribbon. She wasn't wearing any makeup. A stereo was turned down low, playing a violin instrumental of "Penny Lane."

Ginny had already picked the earrings she'd wear tomorrow. She superstitiously wore the same ones for each match until she was either eliminated from the tournament or won it. This pair was long and tubular, like rolled-up hundred-dollar bills, only silver.

"Going to be a nice day tomorrow," I said quietly, not wanting to wake Dirk and Bitsy, even though it was the type of inane comment that was usually shouted heartily at your neighbor over the roar of lawnmowers.

"Checking up on me?" she asked.

"Just doing my job, ma'am. You're up late. You got a match tomorrow."

"Penny Lane" ended; a violin version of "Rocky Mountain High" began.

"Can't sleep?" I asked.

"Haven't even tried yet. It's hopeless. You're out pretty late yourself, walking around in the moonlight."

"I walked over from the cabana."

"Oh, is that right." Half-smiling in a sort of mocking way, she slid her eyes down to my shoes and then up to my face. She tilted her head slightly, and loose strands from her ponytail fell against her shoulder and over her forehead. Her earring touched the top of her shoulder.

"Well," I said, fake-yawning, "I'm going to bed."

"Come here."

"What?"

"Come here."

Her eyes were fixed on me. I felt like my elevator had just dropped thirty stories.

"What for?"

"Because."

For a second I was dizzy and not sure what to do. I had the feeling that Ginny and I had reached the old fork in the road.

I moved toward her. She crossed her legs. Again I noticed the shiny shins, the round bruise. She extended her two slender arms, placed one hand on each side of the computer monitor, and swiveled it to face me.

"What's that?" I asked.

"That's what I'd like you to look at. Will you read it?"

My heart bumped. A letter? To me? A love letter? "Out loud or silently?" I asked her.

She shrugged. "Any way you want. I'm not finished with it, keep that in mind. It's just a rough draft."

As I moved closer to the screen, my nostrils filling with Ginny's bath scent, I silently read:

For several years now my cat BOAT has been a faithful consumer of your product but in recent days since my return home I've noticed a noticed a change in BOAT's preferences when he comes to his

Mealtime he just scratches the floor with his paw,
which in Universal Cat Language means "This is
excrement—bury it" which leads me to belive that
your Company has begun introducing inferior or
adulterated *ingredients into your product and made*
it og

There it stopped.

"Remember," she said, "it's just a rough draft. I haven't proofed it yet."

"It's all one sentence," I said.

"What?"

"It's all one sentence. Look at it. My God, Ginny, it's—there aren't any periods. Don't they teach writing at that tennis academy?"

"You think I should break it up?"

"I think you should dynamite it."

The theme song to "Gone With the Wind" came on. We both looked up at the radio. Dentist-office music or not, when "Gone With the Wind" comes on you can't help but notice. I looked at Ginny and I knew why I had skipped the hamburger and onions: I wanted to kiss her.

But just then the old devil himself, Boat, that goat of a cat, slunk into the room and eyed me menacingly. I'd always had the feeling Boat was plotting ways to murder me; over the years he had made several attempts on my life. For instance, I'd be upstairs in Ginny's house, and he'd lurk near the top of the stairs, waiting for me, and when I started down the stairs, he'd dash out at me and hurl his big overfed body underfoot, trying to trip me. Or I'd be sitting at the table taking a sip of tea or cocoa, and Boat would jump onto the table, swinging his torso against my arm to bump it, trying to make the scalding liquid splash my face.

Even so, I guess I didn't mind Boat. He and I went back a long way.

He leaped onto Ginny's lap. "Ouch, Boat," she said. "Those claws. Mother's been meaning to trim them."

Ginny always referred to herself as "Mother" when she talked to Boat. I got a kick out of that. It was one of those things you either got a kick out of or you didn't.

Petting old Boat and gazing at his face, Ginny said, "She's probably a rich snobby club rat."

"Who is?"

"Antonia Whirlie or Wheelbarrow or whatever her name is. She'll come buzzing into the tennis courts in a red sports car her daddy bought her."

"Yeah, you've said that. You should be plenty used to that type."

Ginny continued stroking the cat's fur, fat Boat purring from the depths of his soul. "Yeah, I'm used to that type. Tennis brats. I'd rather spend my time with—with your runts, for instance. Or with some wholesome, high-spirited youth group."

I laughed. "A wholesome what? Listen, go out there tomorrow and have fun and whack the ball around and have fun."

"That's an attitude for losers."

"That sounds like something Donsprokken would say."

"Well, it's something I say. I do have a mind and thoughts of my own."

"Yes, and I'm real impressed. You sit there saying, 'She'll probably be gorgeous and come buzzing along in her red blah blah blah.' Yep, that's an impressive mind, all right. This ain't a Miss America pageant, you know."

"Now *you're* sounding like Donsprokken."

Boat stretched, jumped off Ginny's lap, came over to me, sidled up to my shins, then abruptly, ferociously, began using my leg as a scratching post. I defended myself. Clamping my mouth shut to keep from crying out, I shoved his front paws away.

"Thanks, fella," I said, rubbing my leg. "Well, I'm going to go home and bandage my leg now. Ginny, you can sit here and fuss and stew the night away if you want, but I'm—"

"Thanks, maybe I will." She turned away from me and repositioned her fingers on the keyboard.

I climbed out the way I had come.

Come here.

How was it that two simple words could have stirred and excited me so much?

I headed to my house through the dark woods, thinking of Ginny. She'd been through so many of these nights-before-matches, you'd think she'd be used to them. And yet she continued to put herself through them. Maybe they were finally starting to wear her down. She didn't run from anything—even something as trivial as writing a letter to a cat-food company. She'd mail that letter. I would have shrugged it off and switched brands.

Was Ginny cracking up? Was she going to fall apart tomorrow and embarrass herself?

My job was to prevent that. But how?

11

"MARK MY WORDS," Ginny was saying. "A red convertible sports car. You wait and see."

We were driving to the club where the tournament was being held. I hadn't gotten much sleep, and that morning I'd had two cinnamon Pop-Tarts and a glass of Ovaltine for breakfast and walked through the woods to Ginny's house, where Bitsy had handed me the keys to her black Jeep Cherokee 4 × 4, which I would be using to chauffeur Ginny to and from her matches. Not a bad deal. Dirk, who had not offered me the use of his Porsche, had taken Ginny's shoulders and squeezed them and said some words to Ginny that I hadn't been able to hear, which Ginny had nodded to. Bitsy, handing me the keys, had looked worried. "Keep her head in it. Don't let her get distracted or out of focus. Don't let her beat herself. Let me know the outcome as soon as possible. Dirk will be out, but I'll be here waiting."

So now, driving along in the Cherokee, Ginny was going on and on about her opponent, and the cinnamon Pop-Tarts were sliding through my intestines.

"Can you let go of it for a while, Ginny?" I said. "Do you have to keep on? You've been going on about it since we left your driveway."

"Donsprokken would have told me to shut up a long time ago."

"Is that what you want?" I said. "Somebody to tell you to shut up and smack you? I thought you wanted to have control of your own mind and life."

She said nothing. I felt bad for losing my patience, for snapping. I gave her a quick look. "Donsprokken tells you to shut up?"

"Yes, and he gets an ugly scowl on his face. Like this." She squinted and grimaced. I laughed. I noticed she was wearing more warpaint than usual. She looked very pretty and fresh and alert despite whatever time she'd finally gone to bed.

"It's worse than a slap in the face," she said.

"What is?"

"Donsprokken's scowl."

"Has he ever done *that*? Smacked you?"

Ginny gave me a wry smile. "Is that any of your business? What would you do if I said yes? Tell me now, honestly, what exactly would you do if I said, Yes, he's smacked me."

"Shake his hand, for starters," I said.

We drove south down the four-lane arterial. The sky was blue, cool, cloudless, the nine o'clock shadows were long and sharp. Ginny fidgeted. Then she'd remember she was fidgeting and relax and do the breathing exercise she'd been taught to ease her nervousness. I wished I'd been taught one.

At a stoplight I snuck another glance at her. She wore light-blue warm-up pants under her white tennis dress and a matching blue warm-up jacket. Her cylindrical earrings dangled. Her hair was pulled back and tied with the same light-blue bow I'd seen last night.

She saw me eyeing her, blinked a few times, and smiled easily. "Hey."

"Hey what?"

"Light's green."

I jumped, and stepped on the gas. After a while Ginny asked me to give her one of my famous patented Claxton pep talks. The kind I gave my team before a big match, guaranteed to pep a person up and shoot vim into them.

"You really want to be pepped up?" I said. "Pep is not a thing to take lightly. Not to mention vim."

"Go ahead, lay it on me. Vim me, babe."

I cleared my throat and gripped the steering wheel. I patted my pockets for a piece of sour-apple bubble gum, but lacking that, I put some extra growl in my voice.

"Tennis is hard," I began. "But it is just. In tennis there is a winner and a loser. It feels good to win and lousy to lose. Nobody wants to be friends with a loser. You lose a tennis match, you have to walk up to the net and shake hands with the gloating, smirking winner. You get home, your mother acts artificially cheerful until you finally tell her to shut up, and then you feel even lousier for hurting her feelings. Your father is quiet, disappointed. You have let him down. Altogether, you feel like a worthless bum. You take a bath a loser, go to bed a loser, get up the next morning— a loser. There are two ways to avoid losing. They are not so hard as you might think. In fact, they are amazingly simple. Number one: Do not hit the ball out of bounds. Number two: Do not hit the ball into the net. There it is. That's the secret. The winner hits the ball over the net and inside the lines; the loser doesn't. Do it pretty or do it ugly, but *keep the ball in the court.*"

Ginny looked at her hands, palms down, fingers splayed. The tops of her hands were tanned, but the fingers were white in between. "Wow. That gave me goose bumps."

"That's pep. With a dash of vim."

"Vim is awesome."

"Believe it, babe."

"The part about the mother and father," she said.

"You weren't by any chance referring to the old days, to *your* mother and father?"

No comment.

We turned into the long, narrow parking strip of the Woodland Club, which today was being used as a loading zone for cars dropping people off, like at the airport. A fussy elderly man, wearing a jaunty hat and a yellow tournament blazer, was importantly directing traffic and pestering people. As soon as he saw me pull over next to the curb, he hurried up to my window, which was already rolled down.

"You can't park here," he said.

"I'm not," I said.

"Looks to me like you're trying to."

"I'm unloading this girl. She has to find out what court she's playing on. I'm her coach."

He sucked his front teeth. "Her what?"

"Her coach."

"Her *coach*."

"Yes, sir," I said.

He looked from Ginny to me and back to Ginny, sucking his teeth, then shook his head. "Poor girl. Go ahead and check in."

I shook my head after he'd left. "Must be on the welcoming committee."

We both got out. I told Ginny I'd stand and wait by the Jeep, just in case the old guy changed his mind and came back to slash the tires.

I watched Ginny make her way through the crowd toward the tournament desk. Lots of people knew her and stopped her along the way. Some of them looked surprised to see her at this tournament.

Leaning against the Cherokee, I tried not to gawk. But the place was swarming with girls. Girls everywhere. Girls in all shapes, sizes, colors, hairdos. As young as six and as old as eighteen. The six-year-olds looked like miniature versions of the eighteens. All different, yet all with one thing in common—well, two things: they were females and they were carrying tennis rackets.

There were girls on their way to their first-round or qualifying match for whichever age group they were entered in, either singles or doubles, carrying their can of tennis balls provided by the tournament desk. Others were returning from their match, trying not to show that they had either won or lost.

Banners prominently promoted the sponsor of the tournament. A female-only product. No boy in his right mind would ever attempt to use that product.

Trying not to think of the female product, I continued to watch the girls go by. The swinging hair, swinging hips, bare legs, knees, calves, pleated or unpleated tennis skirts slapping the backs of bare thighs. Come on, Claxton, get a grip.

Where was Ginny? Had she run off? Slipped out the back? What had I done to be her coach so far? Not much. Delivered my patented Claxton pep talk.

Dropped her off in the loading zone. You lame coach, Claxton. Lame old coach.

It was not the first time it had occurred to me that of all the humiliations Ginny would face this week, perhaps the most degrading was that she had Stan Claxton as her coach.

And maybe that's why Dirk and Bitsy and Donsprokken had gone along with this whole scheme; maybe they *wanted* Ginny to be humiliated. Give her a scare. The way parents made their rebellious kids tour the jail or their cigarette-addicted kids the cancer ward. Here's what will happen to *you* if you don't shape up.

Here's what will happen to you, Ginny. From Rick Donsprokken to Stan Claxton.

Talk about scare tactics.

12

I WAS JUST ABOUT TO leave my car and go looking for Ginny when she finally appeared, walking slowly toward me. Something was wrong.

"What's up?" I asked her.

She shook her head, looking somewhat dazed.

"Which court are you on?" I asked.

No answer.

"Hey, Ginny, how about telling me what court you're on. So I can park the Jeep."

"I'll show you," she said.

"Show me what?"

"Where I'm playing. We have to drive there."

I studied her for a moment. We climbed in the Jeep and I circled around and drove back out of the loading area the way we'd come, past the old man directing traffic.

"What's up, Ginn?"

"Oh, it's not that big a deal, I guess. They told me all the club courts are full, so we have to play our match on a satellite court."

"A satellite court? You mean we have to drive to some off-site court somewhere out in the dingles? You gotta be kidding me."

"They've given me a little mimeographed map, see? Take a left up here."

"What left? There's no street."

"Welcome to the dingles," she said.

I saw a kind of paved driveway or utility road. I braked and turned left onto it and tried to read the map without driving into the trees.

"Kind of pretty in here," Ginny said. "I get to play a match on some rustic court that's probably overrun by beetles. Donsprokken would be popping his cork."

Feeling a bit guilty for not popping my cork, I followed the narrow winding road up and up through the wooded parkland. It really was a pretty park. There were several varieties of massive deciduous trees, purple and violet and yellow wildflowers growing in the grass, dark Douglas firs and pines shooting up to the sky. Another left, which became a dead end after a couple of hundred feet, with a paved turnaround area big enough for three or four cars to park. Ours was the only car. There were picnic tables, a barbecue grill, two garbage cans that looked like they hadn't been emptied since the Korean War. And one lone, cement, fenced-in tennis court.

"Jolly good spot," I said, shifting into Lord Boxton. In my normal voice I added, "At least it's quiet up here; you're away from the hubbub down there."

"About as away as you can get. Gosh, look at the cracks."

"You want me to go back and complain? I'll raise heck if you want me to."

"You're the coach," she said with a shrug. After a pause she added, "I'm terrified."

"Of what?"

"Of today."

"You'll get through it." I wanted to touch her, take her hand.

"My nerves," she said, "are a complete crashing jangle. Why do I put myself through this."

"To reach your maximum something or other," I said. "Let's check out that court. Make sure it's dry. If that's moss on the edge, you ain't playing on moss, I draw the line at moss. Now, about this fear, Ginny. You know you can't listen to your feelings in these situations. Your feelings only want you to be comfortable at the moment, so they feed you all kinds of lies. You have to rely on what you *know*. On your training. And on what your coach tells you. It's that simple."

"Just tell me why I put myself through this," she said again.

"I told you."

"Then why don't you put *yourself* through it?" she said.

"Because I'm a lesser developed human being than you are. On the ladder of moral and spiritual evolution, you're a flamingo and I'm a—a water strider."

She sighed. "I feel myself coming unglued."

"Don't do it inside your mother's Jeep. Now get out and do your stretching."

"Go ahead and say it," she said.

"Say what?"

"I shouldn't have been up all hours last night. I should have eaten my breakfast instead of dumping it in the garbage when Mom wasn't looking."

"Oh, great," I said.

She swallowed. "Man, I think I might even have to throw up."

"Get out there and do your visualizations."

"I visualize throwing up." She opened the door, paused, took a deep breath, and hopped out of the Jeep.

I grabbed the picnic cooler from the back. It was full of food that Donsprokken had instructed me to bring. I took out an orange, thought about peeling it, but changed my mind and tossed it back into the cooler. It struck me that being a coach is like being a den mother organizing a troop picnic.

"All right," Ginny said. "I'll do some visualizations."

"What is it you visualize, anyway?" I asked.

"Balls."

"What kind of balls?"

"Big fuzzy yellow ones floating at me."

"Ah."

"Sailing over the net."

"I get the picture."

"Pausing one by one, mid-flight, so I can hit each one. Don't aim. Don't think about what I'll do after the match. Just a nice easy— By the way"—she looked up at me—"how about we take a dive in the lake after the match?"

"You're a mind reader," I said. "Did you bring a swimsuit?"

"No, but I'll rig something up."

The thought of her rigging up a bathing suit made me catch my breath, but I let it go. "Back to your visualizations," I said. "Big fuzzy balls . . . Big fuzzy balls . . ."

I looked at the tennis court. It was littered with broken bottles and assorted debris. The net sagged in a gentle arc. Like the back of an old sick horse.

There was a sign that said RESERVED ON SPECIAL OCCASIONS FOR TOURNAMENT PLAY. What a laugh. I turned to Ginny. "This is ridiculous. You're not playing on this court. You don't have to stoop to this. I'll go back and raise some heck. If they don't listen to me, I'll call Donsprokken."

Ginny shook her head. "Nah, let's play it. It's just a qualifying match. Nothing to get worked up about. I'll win this tournament just to spite them."

"Now you're talking. Hey! I'm proud of you."

She smiled. "You're just relieved you don't have to raise heck."

"I'll get the push broom."

Ginny looked surprised. "What? You brought the—?"

"Yeah. This morning as I was eating my Pop-Tart it hit me that I'd better bring the push broom. So I grabbed one out of your garage and tossed it in the back. I guess it was a premonition."

"Why, Stan, sometimes you actually impress me."

"Me too. Do your stretching and I'll sweep."

I swept. Broken glass, pine needles, damp leaves, pinecones, twigs, crushed cigarette packages, cigarette butts, dead bees, dead beetles, dead potato bugs, more glass, an apple core. The broom made steady rhythmic scrapes along the asphalt, bringing up puffs of dust and dirt.

Ginny sat on a grassy knoll in the sun, forming S's and V's with her body, and other letters, too. She rolled over on her stomach, kicking up her legs. I felt a stab of compassion for her. She seemed vulnerable. A loss today would be devastating for her. What could I do to help her win?

She rolled back into sitting position, motionless, her legs straight out, her arms behind in support, eyes closed, chin raised. Doing meditations or visualizations or something. Moments later, she tucked her legs into the lotus position, looking relaxed and serene. Earth Princess communing with the sun. Watching big fuzzy balls.

There were still some tiny fragments of glass on the court, so I got down on my knees and began picking them up with my thumb and forefinger. It reminded me of picking diced onions off a pizza.

At last, finished with the court, I went to the parking lot and started sweeping the debris from that. Something to keep busy. I talked to myself, coach to coach: Don't let her beat herself today. Keep her head in it. That's all a coach can do. That's why you're here. No distractions. Don't go distracting her by doing something stupid. Like . . . well, you know, trying to grab her or something. Not today. And yet the mere act of grabbing her did not seem as daunting or monumental as it had last night in her house.

Easy there, Coach. Just keep sweeping. You're here to sweep. To warm her up before her match. Hit with her, put her through her paces. Bring water. Peel oranges. Be there.

That's all we can do for anyone.

13

GINNY AND I TOOK to the court and began
hitting from our hopper full of practice balls. The
court was dappled with sunlight and shadows. Bees
whirred by, wildflowers swayed, Douglas firs gave off
a pungent sweet smell. Ginny was well trained; as we
hit methodically and mechanically, she seemed to be
easing herself to a deeper state of concentration.

"Eeeee yeutch!" she said. Puffs of dust rose from
her strings. She really clobbered that ball. Threw her
whole body into every shot.

I was working hard, sweating, invigorated. Using
my good old Derwint "Derbyshire" XQ-2R-200S.
Pure joy. How simple it was for a tennis racket to
make life fun and worth living. Hitting with my runts,
I seldom was able to work up a sweat. Yet with this
racket, it was fun just being a backboard. I liked the

methodical rhythm of rallying. It was similar to mind-less, manual labor. Like cleaning the toilets. I used to enjoy cleaning the toilets. Your mind free to wander wherever it wanted. My mind was good at wandering. Give it a destination, that's when it got into trouble.

Ginny and I were hitting like the old partners we used to be. Moving each other to and fro in the pre-scribed Donsprokkian patterns. The only thing that threw off our rhythm was when the ball hit a crack and took a bad bounce. I felt fresh and exhilarated, sweat gathering at my brow and the small of my back, my muscles working. My racket supple and alive in my hand.

Ginny paused to go over to the bench and peel off her sweat pants and sweatshirt. I looked away. Looked at the blue sky, the treetops. Better not watch her take off her pants.

We continued our brisk warm-up for another ten minutes. Then we went and sat down on the bench. She wiped her face with a towel. I sat three feet from her on the bench, both ends of which had rotted away. The tops of Ginny's legs glowed pink. As usual, she smelled of soap.

She looked at her skimpy silver watch, then straightened her legs out in front of her. Firm, tanned legs, not muscular, but powerful, like a dancer's. I looked, then didn't look.

"I wonder where she is," Ginny said. "She's not late—yet. Two minutes to 10:30."

"Otherwise known as 10:28," I said.

We sat for a while.

"How about a swig of something, Coach."

Coach reached into the cooler and handed her the plastic bottle of High Tech Sports Training Fluid. In the old days, she'd been satisfied with Gatorade, but evidently this new stuff was state of the art.

"Ah, you're a good coach," she said, taking a swig and handing the bottle back to me. I put my mouth where hers had been and drank. The stuff tasted weaker than Gatorade.

The minutes went by. Ginny checked her watch.

"Twenty-five to eleven," she said. "Androgynous Wheelie is now five minutes late and counting. When she's fifteen minutes late, it's an official forfeit. Except—now get this—they told me at the desk we have to give her an extra eight minutes because of the remoteness of the court. How do you like that? We're supposed to sit here and wait for another—another . . ."

"Eighteen minutes," I said.

"Thank you."

Ginny had a habit of never calling her opponent by her real name but giving it some mangled version. She once told me why she did it. A few times as a kid, the night before a match, Dirk would tell her to include her next day's opponent in her bedtime prayers. She had obeyed, but mutilated the opponent's name to

confuse Heaven. It became a habit, then a super-
stition.

I handed her a peeled orange and worried about
her. She did not like to wait. Waiting sapped her energy. I worried about her lack of sleep last night.
About the breakfast she hadn't eaten. If she had to sit
here and wait the whole eighteen minutes, it could be
dangerous. She could end up beating herself. She'd
done it before.

Maybe someone had advised Antonia Wheeler to
make Ginny wait as long as possible.

One of Ginny's knees had a pine needle stuck to
it. Two bare knees pressed together. Smooth and soft
knees. Not dry and bumpy and hairy like mine. Occasionally she tapped them together, causing her
thighs to jiggle.

Legs. Calves. Gently tapering ankles. Up. Smooth
tanned tops of thighs. Little blond hairs. Hemline—

Geesh, Claxton, get a grip!

For one crazy insane moment I had been tempted
to brush that pine needle off her knee.

I got up and paced. Walk it off, you ninny. I had
seen Ginny in bathing suits, tennis outfits, shorts, Hal-
loween costumes. I had seen her as Cleopatra in a
sixth-grade play. I had rubbed suntan lotion and
mosquito repellent on her shoulders. I had seen her
wearing only a towel. I did not recall ever feeling . . .
flustered.

When she was thirteen she had stopped coming
with us on the ski trips because there was too much
risk of her breaking a leg. I had secretly hated Dirk
and Bitsy for that decision. Or had it been Donsprokken's decision? Or Ginny's?

I turned around and saw her looking at me. She
smiled. "Hey," she said. "Did I thank you for doing
this? For being here? It means a lot to me."

"I'm getting paid handsomely for it."

Why had I said that? Dumb. I walked over to the
High Tech Fluid and took a gulp, spilling some onto
my chest. Overhead, a gang of crows disputed in the
branches.

"You know," Ginny said in a tired voice, "if I lose
this, everyone will say I ought to hang it up. How
pathetic that she didn't even . . ."

Here she goes, I thought. Talking herself into
losing.

"I'm drifting, you know," she said. "Yeah, that's
what I'm doing. Drifting up here." She tapped her
skull. "I don't really know myself, you know. Nothing
about life—"

"Let's hit some serves."

"Nothing about life turns me on. The sun feels
good, though, right here on my face. Well, Anchovia,
the clock is ticking. You're late. I wonder if you're on
your way."

"Probably," I said.

We sat and waited. Five minutes. Five more. Ginny

sat quietly, her nervous energy had evaporated, and I paced, not trusting myself to sit down next to her.

"Looks like she's not showing after all," I said.

"Looks like it." Ginny checked her watch yet again. "Looks like old Andromeda Strain isn't coming. She's forfeited by now, but we'll give her a couple more minutes."

We gave her five more minutes.

"Forfeit," Ginny said. "Antonia Wheeler has officially bit the dust. Even considering the remoteness of the courts."

"Congratulations," I said, patting her shoulder. "How about you and I play a match?"

"Us? We?"

"Yeah. We haven't played a match for years."

"You want to? A real match? A three-setter?"

"You'll kill me in two, but . . . yeah. Let's."

"I wouldn't be too sure I'll kill you," she said.

"Might be interesting to find out."

"All right. But I'm not going easy on you."

"I insist you don't. How about we do this: play a match, work up a good sweat, go to the tournament desk and report the forfeit, find out when and where your next match is, call your mother so she can relax, and then go jump in that lake. Then go get milk shakes. Fresh strawberry shakes. How's that sound?"

"Perfect. Now, you won't get pouty if I beat you," she said.

"I anticipate a good thrashing, and welcome it. You know I don't get pouty."

Somehow I found myself sitting beside her. How had that happened? I grabbed my racket, but we both stayed put on the bench. A tremor passed through me. Before I knew what I was doing, my hand was reaching for her left kneecap. I couldn't stop it. I flicked off the pine needle, then patted the kneecap. Pat pat. A brotherly pat. Not a caress or anything, but the way you might pat your large loyal pet salmon.

A car came. First we heard it. We both turned. There it was, coming into view.

It was red and sporty.

14

"MIGHT NOT BE HER," I said.

"Gimme a break," Ginny said. "It's her."

The car came stealthily, like a prowl car, no sign of hurry or tardiness, and parked a few feet from the Jeep.

The driver got out. Definitely a she. Definite hooters. She was dressed in white—white sport shirt, white shorts, white socks, white canvas sneakers. Sneakers —not tennis shoes. Her skin was milky pale. She had strawberry-blond hair, oodles of it, long and intricately curled and styled, cascading down her back, like a country-singer Barbie doll. She carried one old woody racket in a wooden press, one of those trapezoid presses with wing nuts that screw down, the kind F. Scott Fitzgerald might have used back in the Roaring Twenties. It was the equivalent of showing up at a ski race with wooden skis, cable bindings, and lace boots.

"It doesn't matter whether it's her or not," I said to Ginny. "She's way late. More than half an hour. She's officially forfeited."

The girl approached, smiling, taking long confident strides like . . . well, yes, like a Miss America contestant. "Ginny? I hope I'm not too late for our match."

That was all. No explanation offered.

"That's okay," Ginny said. "You must've had to come a long way."

"Oh, golly, did I. All the way from Woo—Woodinville."

They shook hands.

The girl was smiling eagerly yet vacantly, the perky smile of an airhead in search of a dance partner. What else did that smile remind me of? Where had I seen its type before?

She turned to me for the first time. Our eyes met and there was a perceptible "click."

And so it was. Another girl had entered my life. Taking her place alongside the aerobics instructor, the girl who'd invited me to her birthday party, and the girl who'd pinched me. Four girls who had nothing in common except for one thing: I knew them.

Ginny said, "Antonia, this is Stan Claxton. My friend and coach."

"A real coach? Wolly."

Ginny and I exchanged a look.

Church. That's what the smile reminded me of. You get hit with a smile like that when you enter a church or, as Ginny had put it last night, "a high-spirited upbeat youth group." Welcome! Glad you've come!

I glanced at the racket. The brand was called Flite-Rite. If gum machines were big enough to dispense tennis rackets, that's where this one would have come from. It was worth about ninety-eight cents. On the screw-down press, someone had carved a name—Mary Haynes. A nice name. Who was Mary Haynes? Why had she carved her name on this frame?

The girls took to the court and began warming up. Thirty seconds into the warm-up, it became obvious that Antonia Wheeler, although she had a natural grace and coordination, hadn't had many tennis lessons in her life. Why in God's name had she chosen this tournament, shelled out the money for the entry fee, to play in a qualifying match of a sanctioned U.S. Junior tournament against experienced tournament players, when she would not even have stood much of a chance against half my runts at Sour Lake? I shook my head. Why the new Pontiac Grand Am but the chintzy racket and the clothes that looked like they were from Goodwill?

When I had the opportunity, I muttered ungrammatically to Ginny, "Be merciful. End it quick."

Five minutes into the warm-up, Ginny stopped.

"Hey, Antonia? Mind if I take a look at your racket for a second?"

The two of them walked forward and met at the net. Ginny tapped the racket's frame and plucked the strings.

"Hey, Stan, this is an antique or something. Look at these strings. They're like wet noodles."

I stepped onto the court and examined the racket. "Who's Mary Haynes?" I asked without looking up.

"What?"

"Mary Haynes."

"Oh! Well, I—um—Mary—?"

I shrugged. "Never mind, doesn't matter. Just curious."

Well, that confirmed my suspicion. Antonia or someone had probably bought the racket from a secondhand store.

"Do you—do you really think the racket is that bad?" Antonia asked me.

Ginny and I looked at each other and read each other's mind: Was this person for real? Was this a joke?

Ginny said, "It's barely usable. Don't you agree, Coach?"

My ego was boosted by the way Ginny kept calling on me as an authority. "Yunk," I said, using the Norwegian pronunciation.

"Gosh!"

"You've got such nice form," Ginny said. "You deserve a decent racket. Don't you think she has nice form, Stan?"

"She does," I said. And meant it.

"Believe him," Ginny said. "He knows. He's a top-notch instructor. He knows good strokes and he knows rackets. You ought to see *his* racket. It's the most expensive racket in the world. Made of Twylon and graphite composites."

Not one to be humble about my racket, I went and got it and showed it to Antonia, pointing out some of its key features.

"Whoa, Nellie," Antonia said. "This is some racket." I noticed that her eyes were green, the color of lime sherbet.

"Go ahead and try it," I said. "Hit a few with it. Feel the difference."

"May I really? Oh, jeepers!"

She swung the racket a few times, and then Ginny hit her some balls from the baseline.

"Oh! Ooh! Oh my goodness! This is incredible!"

They rallied for a while. I did not mind letting select people use my racket, so long as the racket didn't leave my sight; I wasn't one of those possessive or jealous guys.

"May I offer you a quick pointer?" I asked her.

"Oh, please do. Oh, yes."

"That left arm of yours. You're letting it dangle limply at your side. I'd like to see you extend that left out in front of you for balance. Like this."

She followed my demonstration, and of course instantly began hitting better. Tennis is, after all, more science than art.

"My goodness, this is just absolutely—! You are a miracle worker. You're a genius. You're the best coach—I ought to hire you. Are you *sure* you don't mind if I use your racket? I'd die if I scraped it."

"I don't think you'd die," I said.

"But, I mean—"

"You won't scrape it if you keep your eye glued to that ball," I said. "That's right. Good one. Hey, you're bending your knees real nice. Nobody ever bends their knees nowadays."

Her legs were plump but pleasing. Her large green eyes didn't blink very often.

Ginny and Antonia appeared to be having a good time, enjoying each other. That was unusual for Ginny, whose shyness people sometimes mistook for snobbishness. The two chatted away as they hit, and they laughed about things they chatted about. It was good to see Ginny laughing, casually stroking tennis balls instead of grunting and trying to knock the cover off them.

"You are a masterful coach!" Antonia shouted to me with laughter in her voice. A voice that was as pretty as her eyes. The voice of an Irish folksinger.

Not one to back away from an apt student, I gave her a few more pointers. They were basic, and they worked. I showed her how to hit volleys and overheads. How to get her serve in and toss the ball the right height. How to put a little topspin on her forehands. Antonia was an ideal pupil; she had no pride. You could give her the most obvious tip and she'd accept it gratefully, without embarrassment. All my coaching instincts came out. And my tennis racket made a difference—it wasn't the most expensive tennis racket in the world for nothing.

"Jeepers, I *love* this!" Antonia shouted. "This is such a high!"

They played a set while I watched from the bench. Or the semblance of a set, as neither paid much attention to keeping an accurate score. Ginny played the way I played with my runts, hitting the ball so it bounced waist-high every time, right back to the middle, not trying to win points but just keeping the rally going, letting the pupil's confidence grow.

When the set and lessons were over, we all shook hands.

"Gosh, thank you both so much," Antonia said. "I feel like I've had a lesson from two masters. Ginny and Stan! This has really been kind of wow!"

We said goodbye. Ginny and I sat on the bench and waved to Antonia as she drove away. She tooted her horn.

I turned to Ginny. "Kind of wow?"

Ginny smiled. "She was genuinely nice."

"A win's a win," I said, shrugging.

"There was something so open and refreshing

about her," Ginny said. "I could see myself being friends with her, even though she's two years older."

"A little on the gushy side," I said. "All those 'jeepers.' But, yeah, nice."

"And pretty, don't you think?"

I made a noncommittal grunt.

"She liked you," Ginny said, looking into my eyes. "I'll bet you didn't notice that, but I could tell. She kept checking you out when you weren't looking. You should have asked her for her phone number."

"You mean to call her up?"

"That's how it's done. That's how you connect with girls, Stan. You ask for their phone number and then call them up."

"How do you know so much about it? Do guys ask you for yours?"

"What, when I'm traveling? No, just my hotel room number. You know, they usually have to go through the hotel switchboard."

"You don't really give your room number to strange guys?"

"Nah, it's simpler just to give them my room key."

I opened my mouth, stopped, opened it again, and Ginny laughed. She bent over and began loosening her shoelaces. "Wasn't that racket of hers a scream?" she said.

"A royal scream," I said. "Speaking of royal . . ." I reached for my racket, but it wasn't on the bench. I looked under the bench. I looked around. Hm. I stood up. I began looking more frantically. My heart leaped into my throat. My blood drained. For a few moments the park fell utterly silent, the birds and squirrels holding their breath and watching me from a safe distance. I wanted to let out an ear-shattering scream. Wanted to but didn't, couldn't. I lowered myself back down to the bench, staring at nothing, at emptiness. All I could do was moan.

15

MY NEXT INSTINCT was to jump in the Jeep
and tear off after her, but she had too big a head start.
At the tournament desk, while Ginny was reporting
her score, I tried Directory Assistance for Woodinville,
but Antonia's number was unlisted, no doubt because
of her rich father. The tournament desk wouldn't give
me her address, so I left my phone number with them
and asked that they call me the minute the racket was
returned. Ginny and I called Bitsy, and then we went
and jumped in the lake.

The water was cool and refreshing. I was wearing
my cutoff sweats and Ginny was wearing a pair of
shorts and a T-shirt.

We swam out to the raft. The sun sparkled off the
water, off the drops on Ginny's eyelashes.

"It was probably an honest mistake," Ginny said. "She'll discover she took it and return it."

"That racket," I kept saying, adopting a slight Lord Boxton accent. "That racket is my whole bloody world."

"Oh, please," Ginny said.

I stared out at the water. Without my Derwint "Derbyshire," I would be cast in a pit. The world would have no zing. Life would be as dull and stale as brushing your teeth without any toothpaste.

Teaching tennis, without that racket, would be dismal.

We were the only ones on the raft. Lying on her back with her eyes closed, Ginny kept saying things like "Fancy her taking it. Oh, stop worrying, she'll figure a way to get it back to you. If she's anything, she's honest. It was an honest mistake. Or no—maybe not a mistake. Maybe she wants you to come after her. For obvious reasons."

"Obvious reasons, bull. She's a thief."

"Thief or not," Ginny said, "didn't you think there was something nice about her? Something real and genuine?"

"She was too nice. It should have tipped me off."

"You're just mad because she stole your racket."

"Gee. How did you figure that out? I'm beyond mad. I want vengeance."

"For a racket you yourself, my dear, acquired

through very shady means. How conveniently you forget."

"Shady means," I muttered, shaking my head.

We dove off the raft and swam to shore and sunned ourselves on the grass. Then we went to Kid Valley for our milk shakes.

The next morning Ginny played her first-round match against an eighteen-year-old college student from Bellingham named Yvonne Tingvahl. She was a giant big-browed blonde with a booming serve and a soft voice and bad posture, probably derived from having towered over every boy she'd ever known. She wore some sort of mysterious white cream over her upper lip. Her personal coach, a thirtyish woman, was also tall and also wore that mysterious smear of white cream over her upper lip. This made the two of them look like weird, spooky sisters.

Yvonne's booming serve was ineffective because her toss was too low. Her groundstrokes seemed cramped. I wanted to tell her to stop being ashamed of her height and start using it: Quit slouching, extend yourself, *reach*. A one-hour lesson with me, I'd've had her serving wickedly. Poor Yvonne. She made so many unforced errors that the spectators yawned and squirmed and stayed only to watch Ginny, who was good enough reason to stay anywhere.

The final score was 6–4, 6–1. Ginny advanced into the second round, where her opponent would be a

Canadian named Pam Gowdy. The match was scheduled for that same day, six o'clock in the afternoon.

"I know Pam Gowdy," Ginny said. "They call her
Barking Pam. She ain't no slouch."

"Why do they call her Barking Pam?"

"You'll see. Poor Yvonne. What do you think the
story was with that cream on her upper lip?"

I shook my head. "Maybe it was some product that
removes unwanted facial hair."

"But her coach had it, too. They wouldn't both be
wearing it, would they?"

"Maybe it was some kind of political statement," I
said. "Remember, they're from Bellingham. Hey,
where'd you get that little angled backhand chip shot
that just skitters over the net?"

Ginny smiled and cocked her head. "You liked that,
eh?"

"That was a thing of beauty. Pure poetry."

"Why, thanks. Nice of you to notice."

"But your line calls, Ginny. Your line calls were
pretty loose. Some of those aces you gave her were
way wide."

"Yeah, well," Ginny said, shrugging, "that's the
trouble with having to call your own lines. If it's a close
call, do you give it to your opponent or to yourself?
When you die, would you rather be known as a tight
line-caller or a loose line-caller?"

"Goody Two-shoes," I muttered.

"What?"

"Nothing. We have six hours until your next match. You wanna go home?"

"No."

"You hungry?"

"No, but I will be. And I know just what I want for lunch."

"What?"

"You'll see."

"Maybe you should go home and rest up," I said.

"Nah. I'd just worry about Barking Pam. I need to take my mind off this tennis stuff. How about we fool around?" She smiled. "Till we get caught. I bet I know what *you'd* like to do."

For some reason, I felt my face go idiotically red. "What?"

"Get your racket back."

"If only I could. That damn tournament desk, they think I'm one of those, you know . . ."

"Stalkers?"

"Yeah, stalker. What a world."

"You wait here," Ginny said. "I'll try my luck."

She headed off through the crowd toward the tournament desk. I stood in the sunshine wondering what she'd want for lunch. Cole slaw? Taco salad? Sushi? Roast-beef sandwich with horseradish?

Minutes later Ginny reappeared, obviously trying to show a poker face to keep me in suspense.

"Brick wall?" I said.

She looked away. "Oh, I don't know about that."

"What did you find out?"

"Simply her address, darling."

"Good girl. Where does she live?"

Ginny held up her index finger with a yellow Post-it stuck to it. "I have it right here. Do you really want to get that racket back, Stan?"

"Yes, Ginny, I do."

"Why? Why does it mean so much to you? Why's it so special? Tell me. You have to give me a good answer or I won't give you this address."

"It's a symbol of my manhood," I said.

"Bull."

"Well, give me some time to think about it," I said. "Let me brood on it awhile. How'd you get it, anyway?"

"The address? Asked for it."

"But how—they just gave it to you?"

"I guess I'm not the stalker type."

"Talk about sex discrimination," I said. "Tell me where she lives. We have six hours to fetch it. I'll buy you lunch on the way."

"All right. I'm easy. It'll be a nice drive out into the country. It's way out past Woodinville. A place called—it's one of those ritzy new developments, you know. A planned community. Called Hai Klickitat."

"Hai Klickitat? I've heard it advertised. A bunch of Seattle Seahawks and Sonics live there. It's ritzy, all right."

"What sort of name do you think that is? Hai Klick-itat. Is it Indian?"

"No, Realtor." I took her arm and led her to the car.

"I can't wait to hear your answer," she said.

"To what?"

"The racket. Why it's so dear to you. Maybe it isn't. Maybe you don't really care about it. Maybe you just want to see Antonia again, to ask her out."

"Yeah, so she can steal my wallet and underpants and whatever else she can get her hands on."

"Like your manhood?"

"That's nondetachable. Are you sure you want to come along?"

"Yes, you might need me to hit her over the head while you grab the racket."

"I'll break her legs, teach her a lesson, that's what I'll do."

"Stan, if she lives in Hai Klickitat, I doubt she's a thief."

"Are you kidding? Haven't you heard of all those twisted rich kids who steal things like lipstick and cheesecloth and panty hose? She's probably rebelling against her nanny."

We drove east in the Cherokee. Out across the windy floating bridge, turning off through Kirkland, going north along the east shoreline of Lake Washington, cutting east again, keeping to the residential streets, zigzagging our way northeast, hitting dead ends, backtracking, skirting parks and bridle trails and shopping malls, farther out in the country, past a trout farm and tree farm and cow pastures and a yuppie winery. In no time I became utterly lost. It seemed as though every development we passed had some computer-selected name—Windsong . . . Party Downs . . . Party Downs II . . . Shorebluff . . . Windbluff . . . Bluffwind . . . Windbreeze—on and on.

The sky was clouding over, the wind gusting. I hoped it wouldn't be blustery for Ginny's six o'clock match. Wind was Ginny's enemy; her game was all finesse and mixed paces, with an array of dropshots, topspins, lobs. That was why she played better on indoor courts or on clay.

We passed about three hundred restaurants and eateries and take-out places, but none appealed to Ginny, who insisted she knew exactly what she wanted but wouldn't tell me until she saw it.

Then she saw it. Good God: a Belgian waffle place. She said she'd been wanting a Belgian waffle since New Year's Eve. She'd been dreaming about Belgian waffles, crispy on the outside, doughy in the middle, heaped with strawberries and whipped cream.

Belgian waffles tended to make me unsettled, like when you're in a theater watching a movie and you suddenly get the feeling you've left your car lights on out in the parking lot.

Then, just as suddenly as she wanted Belgian waf-

fles, Ginny's appetite veered sharply and she com-
manded me to drive on down the boulevard, for she'd
suddenly envisioned something better: the gigantic
Henhouse Supermarket.

A questionable decision. Henhouse Supermarket
had valet parking, shops within shops, a whole global
marketplace within a grocery store. They made me
more nervous than the damn Belgian waffles—harried
checkers, cheeping scanners, tabloid papers, pushy
people, free samples in every aisle, diet books, salad
bars, sushi, tanks full of doomed lobsters, shelves
stocked to the ceiling. A world gone mega.

I told Ginny I'd wait in the car.

"You don't want anything?"

"Nothing."

"Not even a latte?"

"No. I'm too worried about my racket."

While she was gone I drove over to Bill's Chevron
and got gas and a latte. When I came back, Ginny was
waiting for me next to the valet-parking attendants.
Cool and aloof standing there in her short tennis dress,
holding a grocery bag, she looked beautiful and sun-
tanned, every inch of her getting ogled by the four
valet-parking dudes.

I drove up in the Jeep, one of the few times in my
life I've been envied by parking attendants.

"Exciting news," I said as she got in.

"What?"

"Bill's Chevron now offers espresso. There's a two-way speaker on the gas pump. You can order a latte while pumping your gas."

"That sounds like something Guballa would do."

"What does?"

"Pump gas and order a latte from the speaker on the gas pump."

"No," I said. "*Wilcutts* would order a latte. Guballa would make farting noises into the speaker." I tried to see into the sack. "What you got in there? Don't tell me you're going to build your own Belgian waffle from scratch. By the way," I said, "I might as well admit it. I'm lost. I have been for about an hour."

"I knew that."

"How did you know that? I've done my best to disguise it. Pretending to know exactly where I'm going. Making very decisive turns."

"That's what tipped me off. You seemed so sure of where you were going that it could only mean you were so utterly lost that you were picking your streets at random."

To my wonder, she pulled from her sack a container of strawberries, a bag of doughnut holes, and two cold bottles of presweetened iced-tea drink, one of which she handed to me.

"This is livin'," she said. "I'm there selecting my strawberries, and the produce guy comes over and sprays the strawberries with a fine mist."

"That's livin'," I agreed.

She bit lusciously into a strawberry, thus making

strawberry juice. And while chewing the gooey strawberry, she popped two doughnut holes into her mouth.
Her cheeks ballooned.

"That's disgusting," I observed.

"Why? Haven't you ever heard of strawberry short-
cake? It's becoming that inside my mouth."

She had me there. Boy, she had me.

16

IT WAS TWO O'CLOCK. The sky had turned black and rumbly. Ginny and I had stumbled on a green grassy park that seemed to have all the remaining sun of the day shining down on it. We stretched out on the luxurious lawn, drank our iced teas from the bottle, chomped fresh strawberries right up to the green stem, chased them down with sugar-glazed doughnut holes.

Below us were three green-and-red tennis courts, only one being used by two kids, a boy and a girl, about nine or ten, and a tawny Irish setter, busily sniffing. The girl was taller than the boy, and more athletic, but both were hitting well.

"Runts," I said. "Everywhere you go."

"Maybe she'll be a future champion," Ginny said.

"The odds are against it."

"Oh, the odds. Who lives their life by the odds? Look at that backhand of hers, Stan; it's strong. And the follow-through. And see how she gets down? Kids don't want to get down and bend their knees any-more."

"Oh, you just heard me say that to Antonia," I said.

"She's got a nice fluid stroke."

"She could use a few pointers," I said. "Look at that screwy grip."

"Why don't you give her a quick lesson?"

"Because I don't give it out free. I'm a professional. I only do it for money."

"You jaded boy," Ginny said, smiling. "You gave it to Antonia Wheeler free."

"And look what she did. Kyped my racket. Why don't you go down and give that girl one of your rackets? If you're so charitable."

"Maybe I will," she said.

"Yeah, yeah," I muttered.

I was now disgusted with myself, when moments ago I had felt loose and relaxed and close enough to Ginny to be on the verge of who knows what, maybe a touch or a kiss, or telling her about the Whistling Toilets, and had not thought about my lost racket for a whole string of minutes. And now look at me, griping again, about runts, about my racket, about only "doing it" for money, with Ginny calling me jaded and gently getting on my nerves.

"Maybe it's better that we got lost and discovered this park and that pair down there," Ginny said. "Maybe we were led here. Rather than to—to our original destination."

"Led," I grumbled. "By whom? God?"

"Well, He'd be my first choice. But I'm just saying . . . maybe you should let the racket go. After all, you stole it first."

"Stole it! Stole it? My dear, that is a gross exaggeration."

"You committed larceny, what's to exaggerate? You're paying the debt. Your conscience jumps up and bites you every now and then."

"The only debt I'm paying is having to sit here and listen to you yakety-yak and moralize. Why are you such a Goody Two-shoes? What debt do *you* owe? What nasty thing have you done that you're trying to make up for?"

Yawning, Ginny lay back on the grass and gazed up at the building clouds. Her lips were quite accessible, but kissing her now would not be a smart move. Yet those lips looked pillowy and pink in their partial scowl, the fair and pale freckles on her nose, so kissable. All I'd have to do would be to ease myself to her face and . . .

"You used to welcome a good discussion about ethics and conscience," she said. She waited. I said nothing. She continued. "Maybe, deep down, your conscience wanted Antonia to steal your racket."

"Oh, deep down," I groaned. "Who's that talking? Dr. Teresa Ponti?"

"Remember how we used to sit out in the yard at night and look up at the stars and ask all those deep questions?"

"And never get a single answer. Deep questions. They were about as deep as my big toe. 'Where do we go when we die.' 'How come we weren't born hillbillies or Hindus or Chinese or turkeys?' We only *thought* they were deep. All across America, millions of runts were asking those same idiotic questions after their game of Kick the Can or Capture the Flag, and getting back a bunch of dead air. Pretty soon you get tired of asking and give up. Or get religion."

"Some people never stop asking," Ginny said quietly.

"And end up losing their mind," I said.

She thought for a moment. Her voice stayed calm. "People who stop asking, stop wondering about life and meaning and right and wrong, they lose more than that. They lose their soul."

The park was quiet, except for the steady echoing *punk* of the tennis ball that the two runts were hitting on the court below.

Ginny got up, grass blades sticking to the back of her skirt and legs. Where she'd lain, the grass was flattened into a mold of her head and body, but was already springing back up.

"Going down to give them your blessing?" I said. "Or one of your tennis rackets?"

Ignoring me, she went to the Jeep, reached in through the open window, and returned carrying an unopened can of fuchsia-colored tennis balls.

"You're bonkers," I said.

She walked unhurriedly down to the tennis courts. The kids stopped hitting, lowered their rackets. The dog paused from his sniffing to look up.

"You guys could use some new tennis balls," Ginny said. "Yours look pretty dead."

I hoped the runts would tell her to stuff it, but they accepted the can of balls with thanks. The girl immediately popped the sealed top and the air whooshed out.

"Who are you trying to impress, that's what I'd like to know," I said to Ginny as she came walking back. "God? Talk about guilt-ridden. Usually somebody who does all these random acts of kindness, they've got sins they're trying to make up for."

Without even a glance at me, she walked past me and disappeared into the woods.

I let her go. She was weighed down with something, and she needed to go off with it. Hash it out, maybe. I had some hashing of my own to do.

I lay back on the grass and thought of Donsprokken's summer tennis camp. Yes, I was going, and yes, I was taking my racket with me. You better believe it.

I would have that racket. I deserved that damned racket. You needed things like that racket to get you through life. Life, always coming at you, coming at you. One hassle after another.

I had seen the racket two Februarys ago. Ginny and I had volunteered to work at a pro tournament sponsored by Ginny and Donsprokken's club. I was a ball boy and she was a ball girl—not those runts who scurry back and forth along the net, but the ones who stand at the baseline and bounce the ball to the guy serving. It was a good way to see some great pro tennis from about twenty feet away. Plus you got to keep the T-shirt.

The tournament matches were all played at Donsprokken's club, except for two "feature matches" each evening, which were played at the Seattle Center Arena. A tennis court had been laid on top of the hockey rink.

I had been assigned that night to the Arena, and the final match of the night was a well-known Argentine named García playing the Englishman Gerald Boxton, whom nobody had ever heard of.

But I had. One afternoon at the library, leafing through old tennis magazines, I had come across that magazine article about him. It had a photograph of him dressed to go fox hunting, sitting astride his horse in front of his ancestral castle. There was another photo of Boxton playing a match, and the caption commented on his tennis racket. Since then, I had looked for Boxton's name under the Tennis Results in the sports section. He always lost in the first or second round.

That night at the arena, I saw it—the racket. Gray and silver and black, not simply a perfect racket, but otherworldly and futuristic, like Darth Vader's helmet. What would it feel like to pick up that racket and hold it? I could not even imagine.

Gerald Boxton, up close, had looked older than he'd appeared in the photographs. He had short brown hair combed to the side, high ruddy cheekbones, a long, narrow, aristocratic nose. He was surly toward everyone—ball boys, linesmen, umpire, ushers, the crowd, the Argentine—he never smiled. For a rich playboy who dabbled in international tennis for kicks, he seemed awfully grouchy.

The match was a yawner, the crowd gradually thinning out because it was the last match of the evening, a weeknight, people had to go to work in the morning. At ten o'clock Boxton and the Argentine were still duking it out, deuce, add-in, deuce, add-out, an endless third set. Boxton was simply getting more and more pissed off. He groused about line calls, snapped at the umpire, yelled at a fan who sneezed while he was serving, glared at a photographer, and even shot me, his loyal ball boy, a dirty look when I bounced him the ball for his serve.

On match point, after a long rally, Boxton hit his cross-court forehand wide and lost the match. In utter disgust he wound up and flung his racket toward the baseline. It sailed end over end past my head and skidded out of sight under a green curtain.

Boxton shook hands with the victorious Argentine, nodded curtly to the umpire, gathered up his gear at the bench, and stormed off to the locker room. The remaining crowd filed up the stairs to the exits, the ushers followed them, and soon the arena was nearly empty. The clean-up crew came from all directions and began their shift.

I continued to hang around. My ride—a man from the club—would have already left with the other volunteers. The prearranged plan was that if you didn't show up out front by a certain time, it was assumed you'd gotten a ride with someone else.

I moseyed over to the curtain, lifted it, and went under.

I expected the racket to be gone, an usher or someone having been sent to fetch it. But there it was. It had come to a stop against a stack of electrical cord that was coiled inside a hockey net.

I bent down and picked up the racket. It seemed energized; tingling currents shot through my hand and arm. I felt like Luke Skywalker being handed his lightsaber for the first time.

Up to that moment I had not thought about what

I'd do with the racket. Give it to someone in authority. Take it to the locker room myself and hand it to a guard who would see that his lordship got it. Had his lordship even asked about it?

It was so simple to leave through the side exit.

I took the bus home on that mild rainy February night, holding the racket close to me the entire bus ride. When I woke up early the next morning, there it was, resting on my desk next to my computer.

I told no one and showed it to no one, except Ginny, a few days later. She had not been at the arena that night, so I told her all about Boxton and what had happened. She simply listened without comment, maybe figuring I'd return it to the club or something. But I never did. I kept it.

I sat up. Ginny had come back from her walk in the woods and was standing over me, looking down at me.

"All right," I said.

"All right what?"

"All right, I'm a thief. I stole the racket. I admit it."

She made no reply.

"You want to know why I stole it? Why it's so special to me? Well, I'll tell you, Ginny. I stole it because it was there. You tell *me* why certain things happen in

life. Who knows why they happen, they just happen.
Give me one good reason why I shouldn't have taken
it; why I *shouldn't* go get it and keep it now. Because
it's wrong? Tell me why I should choose 'right' over
'wrong.' Why? Does *life* always choose 'right' over
'wrong'? Maybe there's only for or against. *For* Stan
Claxton or against him. My one and only charity is the
Claxton Foundation. I'll tell you something else. I've
stolen other things. I stole Arthur Ashe from the library. I steal from your family."

"Oh?"

"You know that green chair in your parlor? That
heirloom? Every chance I get, I dive under the cush-
ions and pluck out the loose change and pocket it—
direct deposit to the Claxton Foundation. Heck, that
feels more like stealing than taking the racket did.
Taking the racket, that felt like accepting a gift, pure
and simple, picking up something an obnoxious guy
had thrown away. And it still does feel like a gift, and
I still want it, and I'll want it until God comes and
takes it away from me Himself—instead of using some
pawn like Antonia to do it."

I had said enough. I waited for Ginny to say something. For a while she looked at me with her eyebrows
slightly raised. Maybe she had wanted to make her
own confession; she was holding something in, but
now there seemed to be a huge distance between us,
and she said nothing.

We headed for the Jeep. The kids on the tennis

court, seeing that we were leaving, called thanks to Ginny, and Ginny waved at them.

Finally, all she said to me was "You still insist on going after it, then?"

"I insist."

17

A HALF HOUR LATER we drove into downtown Woodinville. I took a wrong turn through the
crowded business district and found myself on a street
that said FOR PEDESTRIANS ONLY. Fortunately, there
were no pedestrians (or cops) around. It proved to be
a shortcut to a curvy wooded road that took us past
several developments and eventually to Hai Klickitat.
We drove past cul-de-sacs in different stages of development, from empty lots to finished, fully landscaped residences; past Hai Klickitat Elementary
School, still under construction; and past a lavishly
equipped children's playground, deserted except for a
couple of crows perched atop the bright orange swing
set. I had to take a leak. Ginny waited in the Jeep
while I plunged into some bushes and hacked my way

through twigs and spiderwebs and found a nice secluded spot that needed hosing down. When I came
back to the Jeep, Ginny handed me one of her indi-
vidually packaged moist towelettes, which she habi-
tually hoarded from airplanes and fish 'n' chips bars.
She never went anywhere without handfuls of them in
her bag. As I tore open the packet and unfolded the
moist lemon-scented towelette, I noticed she was
looking at me.

"What?" I said.

"You have dead bugs all over you."

"Oh."

Down two more streets, and finally, at the end of
a cul-de-sac, three hours and twenty minutes after
starting out from the Woodland Club, we found our
destination: Antonia's mammoth house.

The driveway was empty and I couldn't see if there
were any cars inside the garage. The house had a deserted look.

I left the Jeep parked beside the curb. Ginny opted
to stay in the car, her window rolled down and her
right elbow poking out.

I pushed the doorbell at three politely spaced in-
tervals, but no one answered. I walked around the side
of the house, unlatched a gate, and went into the back
yard, hoping the Wheelers did not raise pit bulls. It
was a small back yard in proportion to the size of the
house, but I heard, and then saw, a pleasant artificial

waterfall in one corner of the garden. A three-tiered wooden deck looked out on a wooded gully. On the top tier I found Antonia.

She was sitting in a lawn chair, wearing portable cassette headphones and big oval sunglasses, like Jackie Kennedy's. A spiral notebook lay open face-down on her belly button. She appeared to be snoozing. If my life were a movie, she would have been not snoozing but dead, a neat bullet hole between her wide glassy eyes. Or snoozing but stark naked.

She was wearing pink running shorts and a man's button-down workshirt tied in a knot above her belly button, the sleeves rolled up to her elbows. No tennis racket was in sight. The waterfall splashed harmoniously. I felt a few raindrops from the sky.

I cleared my throat. "Sorry—uh—to disturb you. It's Stan Claxton, come to get my racket. That racket is extremely—it means everything to me. I'm sorry to disturb you."

Antonia sat up, removed her sunglasses, and slipped off her headphones. She stared placidly at me for a full ten seconds, which is a long time to be stared at.

More fat raindrops hit the deck. The wind picked up. Antonia said, "I'm glad you've come. How resourceful of you. Will you come in for a second?"

"You don't have a gun in there, do you?"

She smiled, but didn't deny it. "Come in for a minute."

She was different from how she'd been at the tennis courts. Less cheery, more laid-back and . . . sedated.

She stood up and yanked at her shorts the way girls do, and stretched contentedly. Her joints made a cracking sound. The raindrops were increasing, bringing out a sweet damp cedar smell from the deck. It occurred to me that Ginny's six o'clock match might get rained out.

Antonia opened the door and led me inside her house. Where any kind of weird thing could be waiting. Maybe a half-eaten corpse on the living-room floor, or a pentagram for satanic rituals, or a Barbie doll collection.

Of course, if this were a movie, starring somebody like Gerald Boxton, she'd be leading me to her bedroom, which would have a full-length mirror on the ceiling, positioned over the bed.

She stopped in what was apparently the family room, which had a big-screen TV, a multimedia center, a fireplace with numerous family photographs on the mantel, and artwork on all the walls. A deep white carpet; magazines and coffee-table books neatly arranged. There was something artificial and museumlike about this family room.

"My father and stepmother," she said, stretching again, "are in Orlando."

"Disney World?" I asked.

"Hm?" She crossed the room to the window. "That your Jeep down there?"

"It's Ginny's mother's."

Still looking out the window, she asked, "Are you guys a thing or something?"

"Who? Me and Ginny's mother?"

"You and Ginny. I get the feeling you're not. But there's something strange about that, because you'd make an incredibly attractive couple if you were. So there's something not quite right." She turned and faced me with sultry, half-closed eyes and parted lips, like Ginger on *Gilligan's Island.*

I said in a tight voice that didn't sound like me, "If your parents are in Orlando, then—"

"—then I'm all alone. You know, you were so nice the other day when you gave me lessons. You were really, oh—proud, you know? You had something to give me, and you were enjoying giving it but trying not to act like you were enjoying it. Like—like there was some urge in you forcing you to do it. You were so nice to me—both you and Ginny were. I'm not used to people being so kind. People tend to be cruel and selfish, don't you think? There's so much evil. Do you think she'll win it?"

"Ginny? The tournament? No, but she's got a shot."

"My father says tennis is a wimpy game. He prefers killing animals."

"Is that why he went to Orlando?"

She laughed. "That's a good one. Do you live in Seattle, Stan?"

"Yes."

"There is so much . . . so much strife and crap in the city."

"It's everywhere," I said.

"Not here! Not in Hai Klickitat!" she said gaily. "We're fully protected. Can I get you something to drink?"

"No, thanks. I had a latte and an iced tea."

"Then you must be thirsty."

"Uh, no."

"Do you think it'll be the rich, beautiful people who will inherit the earth, Stan? Instead of the meek?"

I scratched my head. "Am I missing something here?"

She grinned. "Oh, we rich, beautiful people, we think we're fully protected and insulated. All our cars and houses will have bulletproof windows and everything. But it's all a delusion. There will be roaming gangs. Urban war—drug lord warring against drug lord. They'll hit every neighborhood and suburb, raping and pillaging. It'll be like medieval times. The houses will grow bigger—fortresses, Stan, each walled-in community a fortress, with unemployed loggers and fishermen and farmers working as security guards. But nature will come back and reclaim everything, Stan. Nothing can protect us from nature. Earthquakes, fires, floods, storms, drought. *That's* what will inherit the earth."

When she finished, she was breathing hard. I stood there wondering what to say. Finally, I cleared my throat and said, glancing toward the window, "Speaking of nature, I wonder what it's doing out there."

She laughed. "You're so cute. When you showed up just now? I'd been listening to a tape I made of some songs I wrote myself. My own songs. There's this one song I wrote," she said. "I just—I need someone's reaction. Would you mind if I sing it for you?"

She left the room. I waited. I tried to calculate the odds of Antonia coming back to the room naked, or in a see-through negligee. Long odds, I guess. I had to face it; my life would not make a good movie. I would never be an international playboy who dabbled in things. I was strictly small-time. Minor league.

I went over to the window and looked out. Through the rain I saw Ginny, her eyes closed, the nape of her neck nuzzled against the headrest. Her tanned arm stuck out in a V, getting rained on. Why didn't she roll up the window? That was her tennis arm. She ought to be keeping it covered, like pitchers do.

Antonia came back, still fully clothed. She now had a guitar. She swung the strap around her neck, hefted the guitar, and began to tune it. She said, "Here's the song I want you to hear." She began to strum, and she sang in a soft, breathy voice:

The gift of the silver harvest
Is coming through for you today.
The gift of the silver harvest
Is coming through for you
Today.

She had a sweet, tender, wispy voice. It was the voice not so much of an Irish folksinger, as had been my impression yesterday, but more like that of Shelley Fabares singing "Johnny Angel."

The words of the song were simple enough—harvests and other spiritual stuff. But the tune—the tune struck me. I recognized it instantly. It was from a perfume commercial on TV about five years ago.

"What do you think?" she asked when she finished.

"Very pretty," I said. "But . . ."

"But what? Go ahead. You can be honest. I respect your opinion."

"Well, the tune. It's from an old perfume commercial on TV. A perfume called Brucie. I don't remember all the words, but it went something like—" I cleared my throat and sang:

Something of the wind in a new young fragrance
That's kinda wow for today's new you;
You know who the You in you is,
And I think you do—
It's Brucie.

Antonia stared at me in shock for a long time, not blinking. Finally, without a word, she took her guitar and left the room.

She was gone for several minutes. When she came back, she had no guitar.

"You're the first *Stan* I've ever known," she said in a loud, overdramatic voice. "If you had another *A* you'd be *Satan*. One letter away. Did *that* ever occur to you?"

"Almost daily," I said.

She brushed some of her wavy hair out of her face.

"Antonia, about that song," I ventured. "Your words are certainly better than that lousy perfume company's."

"Hell, I stole them, too," she said.

There was a rumble of thunder outside. The room had grown dark. Rain beat against the windows. Surely Ginny had rolled up her window by now.

"I'd better get going," I said.

Antonia said, "I'm expecting a call from Clint Eastwood."

"Well," I said, nodding, "I won't keep you, then. Do you—uh—do you by any chance know where that racket is?"

"I was going to give you my phone number yesterday and ask you to call me, maybe give me some lessons or something. Only I was too shy. And Ginny was there. It would have been tacky for me to—well, if you two were—so I swiped your racket. I figured you'd find a way to find me, if you were resourceful enough. I like resourceful boys. I love the whole concept of resourcefulness. I love reading novels where enterprising boys start their own dog-food delivery business and things like that. Would you care for some homemade ice cream? Don't leave. Would you like to go downstairs? Would you?"

Downstairs?

"I need to get going," I said.

The phone rang. It wasn't a ring but the high-pitched chirp of a cordless phone. Antonia picked it up and zipped out the antenna. "Hello? Oh, hi. Ahhh! No way. Really. Oh, yes. Yes. Goody. Oh, yes, is that a great success?"

The conversation lasted another inscrutable minute before she finally hung up. "That was Clint Eastwood."

"Ah," I said, nodding.

"He and my father go fishing in Alaska on my father's boat sometimes. Downstairs there's a picture of them with a giant halibut. Wait here, I'll go get the tennis racket."

She was gone another couple of minutes. I waited. I heard the rain and heard her footsteps upstairs. She was nuts. She was probably getting the gun or hatchet or cattle prod or whatever she intended to use on me. She'd come back and kill me. Or her father, who

thought tennis a wimpy game, would come walking in,
find this stranger in the house with his daughter, and
kill me.

She came back. She had the racket in her left hand
and an object in her right hand which I couldn't see
because she was hiding it behind her back.

"Listen, Stan—gosh, you have the nicest eyes. Listen, I *am* sorry I took the racket. I don't have any
excuse. I can't blame anyone. I have a very good
friend, really only one good friend, but I haven't seen
her for a while, she moved away, she's nineteen, a year
older than me, and we knew each other from the Cal-
ifornia days. She's a ballerina—a world-class ballerina,
she's in one of the most famous ballets in the world.
Not a major star or anything, but they've been touring
all over the world, and they're coming to Seattle.
That's why Clint called—he and I are going 'cause my
parents can't make it. I can get you on the Pass List.
You could take a date—Ginny or someone else. I was
thinking I'd call her up, this good friend of mine, her
name's Mary Haynes, and she'd put you on the Pass
List. You and a date. Stan, believe me, tickets to this
ballet are like gold—people are going crazy to get
them—it's been sold out over a year. But I'll have
Mary see to it that your name's on a list at the Will
Call window, the night of the performance, which is
this coming Monday. I would like to give you tickets,
as a gift to you and Ginny. For being nice people, for

caring, for my ripping you off after you were so nice to me and for—for being my friend. You and Ginny both. And I'd also like to give you this."

She swung her arm out at me. My first instinct was to dive, thinking it was a gun or a knife. But it was an offering of some sort. It looked like the paw of a rodent.

"What is it?" I asked.

"It's the paw of a kangaroo."

"Well," I said.

"Take it. For listening to my song. For being honest. Please take it. See? One end is a kangaroo paw, which makes a handy back scratcher, and the other end is a can opener. If you'll tell me your last name, I'll put you on the list. You'll never see another ballet like this in your life, Stan, you'll be able to die happy after you see this ballet. Is your last name Clapton?"

"Claxton."

"Oh, that's right. Clapton's the Eric. Well, goodbye, friend. Tell Ginny, best of luck in the rest of the tournament. Can you find the door? I'm expecting a *rather* special phone call and I'm going to take it in the Jacuzzi."

Outside, it was raining lightly. When I got to the car, carrying the racket and the paw, Ginny sat up. I started the car, turned on the wipers, and drove off down the street.

"Sorry I took so long," I said.

"That's all right. Mission accomplished?" She looked into my eyes. "You *were* kind of a long time. Did anything—um—happen?"

I glanced at her, unable to fathom what she meant by that. I said nothing, leaving it to her imagination.

"What's that?" Ginny asked.

"That? That's a kangaroo paw." I handed it to her.

"Just what the world needs," she said. "A kangaroo paw can opener. Looks like it'd make a good back scratcher."

"That's what *she* suggested."

Ginny gave it a try.

18

WE WERE ON OUR WAY back through downtown Woodinville. Cars had turned their headlights
on. I pulled over to a phone booth in the parking lot
of a Dairy Queen, so Ginny could telephone the tournament desk to see if her six o'clock match was going
to be rained out. A sign on the bank building across
the street blinked 61 degrees, 3:56 p.m.

"Almost forgot I had a match," Ginny said. "It
shows how well you're doing your job. Only trouble
is, I don't know the phone number of the tournament
desk."

"Hm, that is a problem," I said, stroking my chin.
"But a coach, Ginny, comes prepared." I whipped out
my wallet, flipped it open, and plucked from it the
white card on which Donsprokken had written the
phone number of the tournament desk.

Ginny, suitably awed, took the card from me. She had put on a light-blue hooded rain slicker, and she raised the hood and dashed out into the downpour to the phone booth, which I now noticed had no door or roof. I stayed in the Jeep, my thoughts skipping around. If I lived to be an old man, would I remember this day—the trip to Antonia Wheeler's house? Would I still have the Boxton racket, probably a valuable antique by then? Would I remember Ginny?

I watched the clear raindrops course down the windshield, and shivered. I pictured myself, red all over, taking a Jacuzzi with Antonia Wheeler. Then I pictured Clint Eastwood doing it. I saw Antonia's seductive half-closed eyes. Had she been coming on to me? No girl had ever told me I was "cute." Pinched me, yes; made a pornographic gesture from a bent-over position, yes. What would a normal healthy sixteen-year-old male in Nashville or Kenya or Buenos Aires have done in the situation I had found myself in with Antonia Wheeler? Followed her downstairs? Whipped out his wallet and plucked out a condom?

Through the blurry windshield I saw the hooded Ginny standing at the pay phone, holding the phone in one hand and her calling credit card in the other, getting rained on. Her trim, sturdy bare legs went up and up into the rain jacket, making it look as if she wasn't wearing anything underneath. She was like a little kid, standing there talking into the phone and swiveling from side to side. All alone. The day had become so bleak. I suddenly felt bleak and lonely inside, like you feel the night before the first day of school.

Why did life keep coming at you? Why couldn't it ever back off and give you a rest? The Whistling Toilets gave some moments of peace. Hai Klickitat was insulated and secure. But perhaps the most insulated place you could find would be Donsprokken's summer camp. That would be a real retreat. That was the place to be.

Ginny finally hung up and made her way back to the Jeep. "Well," she said, climbing in, "their rule is, they don't make a decision about postponing a match until an hour before the match. So for mine we have to wait until five o'clock."

"What's it doing in Seattle now?"

"Raining like mad, they said. But if the sun comes out, the courts can dry up in a snap."

"It's 4:08. We'd better head back," I said.

"It's frustrating."

"What is?"

"Trying to play tennis in Seattle."

"Oh. Yeah." I gave her a quick glance. My mood had changed and it seemed hers had, too. Something in her voice or face was different. I didn't start the ignition. "Everything okay?" I asked.

She looked at her lap. "Oh, I do have some news."

Some news. This did not sound good. What did I tell you? Life, you just don't let up. She's going to lay something on me. The confession. The boyfriend tennis twerp.

I still didn't start the motor. We stayed in the Dairy Queen parking lot, rain drumming the roof. I didn't want to know. But I had to know.

Ginny didn't look at me. "After I called the tournament desk," she said, "I called my mom."

"Oh?"

"Donsprokken's coming."

"Here?"

"He's arriving late tonight. He's taking it for granted that I'll beat Barking Pam, and he wants to watch my quarter-final match against Kim Korticek. He's going to stay for the rest of the tournament."

"What about St. Louis? The team?"

"Well, I guess he figures he can leave them on their own."

"Coming all this way. Hm. Kim Korticek must be something."

"She is. She's special. *If* we play each other, it'll be a big, big match for both of us. We've never played each other before. She's a shooter."

"A what?"

"A shooting star. An up-and-comer. Only thirteen years old."

Shooter. Ginny's Scrabble word the other day, before she'd changed it to hooters. "Only thirteen?" I said. "And she's entered in the eighteen and unders? I've heard of playing up, but that's ridiculous. Will

Donsprokken want to take over as your coach when he gets here?"

"He'll want that, yes. That's the way he is, always gotta step in and take over. But what he wants isn't necessarily what he's going to get. It's up to you."

I looked at Ginny. "Donsprokken said that?"

"I don't know what he said; I only talked to my mother. I'm saying, it's up to you whether you stay as my coach."

We were silent for a while, listening to the rain. Ginny had picked up the kangaroo paw and was rubbing her finger back and forth along its short gray fur.

"Up to me, eh?"

"Yeah."

"Well, there's something I need to know."

"What?"

"I don't *want* to know it. And I sure don't *demand* to know it. I wouldn't say I have any *right* to know it. If you don't want to tell me, that's fine. I'll step down as your coach."

"What is it you want to know?"

"I told you, I don't wa—"

She squeezed her eyes shut. "Yes, yes, I got that. What is it, Stan?"

"What's going on, Ginny? Is it you and Donsprokken? Or you and . . ."

Ginny continued to rub the kangaroo paw. I sat there bracing myself. The windows were fogging up. Finally, she said, "I don't know which is more unbelievable. The part about Clint Eastwood calling her or the ballet. That ballet, you know, my parents would *kill* for tickets to it. I hear it's been sold out a whole year."

"Yeah, that's what Antonia said."

"We were having a great day, weren't we," Ginny said. "Funny how you and I can spend a day together and have it end up so fun and different and—and memorable. I've wrecked it. I shouldn't have called my mother. That was a—that was a dumb move."

"No," I said. "Something hasn't been right. It's been here between us the whole time—since you've been home. I've felt it."

"You have?"

"Yes."

She turned away, but I could see her eyes, cold and shining. Damp strands of hair stuck to her forehead. She fingered the kangaroo paw.

"He came on to me," she said.

"He. Donsprokken?"

"Yes."

"Made a pass?"

"Kissed me."

"What did you do?"

"Before, during, or after?"

"Let's try after."

"After . . . I went back to reading my book."

"Where were you?"

"At the outdoor pool. Hilton Hotel. This was, oh,

two months ago. He came up to me and asked me what I was reading and then he—he leaned down and—"

"Poolside. We're talking bathing suits here?"

"Yes, bathing suits."

"This was a public place? Broad daylight?"

"Daylight, but nobody around. Not a soul. Totally deserted."

"So he leaned down and he—he put his lips on you."

"Otherwise known as kissing."

"How long?"

"The kiss? Oh . . . long."

"Long? What's long? Half a minute? Half an hour?"

"Somewhere in between."

"That's not a kiss. That's a prolonged series of kisses."

"Yes. Prolonged."

"Also known as heavy petting."

"Okay."

"Did he put his paws on you?"

"Yes."

"Where?"

"All over."

"His hands? Everywhere?"

"Yes. Even my book."

"When he finished, you picked the book back up and started reading it again?"

"Pretended to, yes."

"What book?"

The Diary of Anne Frank."

"*Anne Fr*—I thought you read that in sixth grade?"

"I did. I was reading it again."

"What did *he* do after?"

"After? He sort of bowed his head and—h-hung his head."

"In shame?"

"Yes. Apologized."

"Profusely?"

"No, not profusely. He said he was sorry, he couldn't help himself, he didn't know what had come over him. I wouldn't call it profuse."

"Did you touch *him*?"

"During? Yes. Put my arms around him."

"How could you put your arms around him with the—I mean, what did you do with *Anne Frank*?"

"She slid off my lap."

I shook my head. "Donsprokken. That bucket of sputum. Do you—are you—do you have the hots for him?"

She hesitated, took a breath. "I've had a crush on him for a long time. I mean, a *long* time. I've had to think a lot about my motivation, for playing tennis, I mean, for dedicating myself to tennis. Part of me has always believed I could have him. The past few months, things were getting a little more, well, everything, you know, has a way of heating up. It wasn't just some accidental moment at that poolside. I'd been flirting for who knows how long. It's been distracting me from tennis, I suppose. I've cared less about tennis these past months. And then when he— Well, it was stupid. It was pretty pleasurable but stupid—we both were stupid. It's over. I am *not* going to make a big deal out of it. I'm not going to blow the whistle and tell anybody—except you—and make it a big issue. I don't want to be a victim. I'm *not* a victim. He didn't take advantage. We were both stupid. That doesn't excuse us. But it's done. It's gone. Deleted. No lasting effect."

"No lasting effect? Then why has your tennis game sucked lately?"

She didn't answer.

"And why did you tell me, if you've deleted it?"

No answer. She was biting her lower lip.

"And why is it you find out he's coming and all of a sudden you say our day is ruined? And what about the other girls on the team? Suppose he tries to maul somebody else? Or already has? Or do you think you're just special to him because you flirted with him. Poor innocent guy."

She shook her head. "I'm sorry . . ."

I laughed. "What?"

"I'm sorry, extremely sorry, I told you. I thought I could tell you, but I was mistaken. Gee whiz. I didn't think you'd react like such a . . . such a *guy*."

"I'm not reacting like a guy."

"Yes, you are."

"Well, I don't like seeing other guys mauling every teenage girl he can lay his paws on."

"He didn't maul me and he's not pawing every—"

"Okay, okay, just you, eh? You're special to him."

She shook her head. "I don't flatter myself to think— Oh well, maybe I flatter myself, just a little. Other girls? I suppose he's capable of grabbing other girls. But I don't think he will. I don't think he's . . . predatory. I'm not a victim. He's the one who's scared. He and I need each other. If I want to move ahead in my tennis, I need him as my coach."

"You haven't moved ahead in tennis. You've fallen back."

"Well, I—I certainly don't want to destroy his career. I was partly to blame."

"For what? Reading *Anne Frank*?"

"For being infatuated with him. And letting it show more than I—for being aware of letting it show. Sending signals. He's done a lot for me, Stan, over the years. He's a friend. I've known him since I was six— only a year less than I've known you. He's been my *coach*. I don't know what the right thing is. Drop him? Ruin him? Does that serve any purpose? I don't want to ruin him. It's all very confusing and complicated, but I'm not looking for advice."

"What are you looking for, then?"

She thought. "A friend. A best friend."

Now she was doing something I hadn't seen her do

since fourth grade: gnawing her thumbnail. Her eyes darted up to me.

"Are you—do you think less of me now?" she asked.

"Less of you?"

"Are you disgusted?"

"Disgusted . . . Ginny, I'm sitting here with stolen property in my back seat. What right have I got to be disgusted with anybody?"

"How about flaky and goofy, then? Do you think I led him on? Do you think I'm tainted?"

"Tainted. Hell. Who isn't tainted. Look, Ginny, there's something I've wanted to tell *you*. But I can't right now. There isn't time. And it has to be the right time. But I just want to let you know. And I need to show it to you."

"Can't you give me a hint?"

"No."

"Is it good or bad?"

"I don't know. It's neither. It just is. It's something you'd show your best friend. I won't say any more right now. We have to get going. That darn bridge is probably backed up."

19

GINNY'S SECOND-ROUND MATCH against
Barking Pam Gowdy didn't get rained out; the sun
broke through and the wind dried the courts. In this
round the players still had to call their own lines, and
Barking Pam, instead of calling "Out!" when a ball was
long or wide, emitted an inhuman "Aaoop!" It made
the spectators chuckle. To my ears, it was more a yelp
than a bark.

Ginny was in good form, though she had to adjust
her game to the irregular wind and to Pam's yelps.
She started out ploddingly, down 3–4 in the first set,
then pulled even, then hit a barrage of winners that
left Pam barkless, and took the first set 6–4. After that,
Ginny caught fire and the crowd caught it along with
her, and Pam grew vague, as if she were mentally
making a list of things to do when she got back to

Canada. Final score: 6–4, 6–2; Ginny advanced into the quarterfinal round to play Kim Korticek at two o'clock the next day.

That evening Ginny called me to say that Donsprokken had arrived. There'd been a big discussion in Dirk and Bitsy's den. Donsprokken had insisted on relieving me of my coaching duties and taking over. Dirk and Bitsy had backed him up. But Ginny (according to Ginny, of course) had resisted, arguing that it was unethical, not to mention unlucky, to replace your coach in the middle of a tournament. That had won her the argument.

So once again, around noon the next day and for the fourth time, I drove Ginny to the tournament. She still wore her same cylindrical earrings and a touch too much warpaint, and today's ribbon color for tying her hair was purple.

On the way, I asked her about Kim Korticek. Ginny told me Kim was originally from Scranton, Pennsylvania, but now living year-round at one of the best academies in western Florida and working with a top-notch coach. On the fast track to the pros, she'd been written up in several magazines and had all kinds of sponsors wanting her to sign on the dotted line.

"Sounds a little like you," I said.

"A couple of minor differences," Ginny said. "She's two years younger and on the way up. While I'm sort of, well, ahem. Plateauing?"

"Think you can beat her?"

Ginny smiled. "Ho ho ho."

"What does that mean? Ho ho ho, yes, or ho ho ho, not a chance?"

"It means at this moment I'd like to be up at the cabin, sitting beside some remote lake that I've just hiked seven miles to, watching the fish jump, with no butterflies in my stomach and no thoughts about anything."

We arrived at the courts early, checked in, waited near the scheduled court where a match was finishing up. It was crowded and hectic. Time passed slowly and Ginny was quiet, not at all fidgety, which worried me. Where was all the nervous energy?

She nudged me and nodded toward a cluster of people a few feet away, in the center of which was a scrawny, frightened-looking girl, a pale version of Audrey Hepburn in *My Fair Lady*.

"That's Korticek?" I said. "You gotta be kidding me. She looks like a frightened fawn."

"That big hairy guy standing next to her is her coach. He's from Romania. He's coached some biggies."

"Who are all those other people?"

"Oh, you know, her entourage."

"She's like some frail princess," I said.

"That's a pretty way to put it. I like that better than frightened fawn."

"Actually," I said, "more like a frail princess who's been abducted by a weird cult and brainwashed."

"Those're the toughest to beat," Ginny said. "The abducted brainwashed ones."

I looked at her. "How're you doing? You feel ready? You're too calm. That scares me. I haven't been tempted to slap you once all day. You ought to be annoying instead of quiet and subdued. Makes me think you're giving up before you start."

"Relax, Coach. You're the one all keyed up. I feel all right. Why don't you do some visualizations?"

"Tell me why you're different," I said. "What's changed? Is it that you're playing somebody younger, an up-and-comer? Is it something about yesterday? Is it that Donsprokken's here now?"

"Look," Ginny said, "I'm about ready to slap *you*."

I felt helpless and useless, but the least I could do was shut up. I looked over at Kim Korticek. Her entourage fluttered about her busily and ineffectually, so that Kim seemed to be the center of attention while at the same time completely isolated. This reminded me of an old black-and-white silent movie I had seen in school last year, about Joan of Arc, who'd claimed to hear the voice of God. She'd sat in the French courtroom with a divine serenity and stillness, while her judges and accusers eddied about her and ragged on her. You half-expected her to levitate above everybody.

"What are you thinking about?" Ginny asked me.

"Joan of Arc. How about you?"

"Me? I was wondering what, actually, sputum is? What would it look like in a bucket?"

"I'll tell you sometime over dinner. You'd better confine your thoughts to this match right here and now, girl. You're about to play a thirteen-year-old tennis robot who has traveled three thousand miles to play in this tournament. Are you interested in beating her or not?"

Ginny sighed. "Stan, look at her."

"Yeah?"

"Take a good hard look."

"Yeah?"

"That's me, two years ago. Now keep looking, keep looking. Do you see it?"

"See what?"

"It's right there for anyone to see."

"What is? I don't see anything."

"Her soul. All fluttering and tattered. Hey," Ginny said, patting my hairy knee, "don't you worry about me. I'll be okay." She got up and walked a few feet away and began listlessly doing some stretching exercises.

It suddenly hit me that Ginny was going to lose, and that she knew it. She had resigned herself to it.

Could it be? Could that thirteen-year-old standing over there really be that tough?

I looked hard for Kim Korticek's soul, but her face intrigued me more. She had one of those scared, narrow, pale, heavily made-up faces that you see on Olympic gymnasts. She never closed her mouth; she looked too frail and weak to breathe through her nose or do anything except fancy-dance atop a balance beam. She looked like she couldn't even hold a tennis racket, let alone swing one, and in fact someone in her entourage was holding her stack of rackets. Kim Korticek held only herself, hugged herself as if she were her own dolly.

Then Kim screwed up her face as if she were about to cry and said something, and the people in her entourage snapped to alert and searched frantically through bags and pockets until at last somebody produced a giant yellow bag of peanut M&M's, and someone else, whose job was feeder, handed Kim a few pellets at a time and she sucked them poutily, unblinking, while her big bear of a coach talked soothingly into her ear.

Kim's eyes landed on mine. Our eyes met for a couple of beats. I saw how ghostly pale her face was, the purple crescents under her eyes, and I might have caught a glimpse of her soul.

I winked at her. Her face, in response, clouded over, and she averted her eyes, but I kept looking at her, because I knew she was going to look back at me. When she did, I winked again. She turned red and became flustered, though obviously trying not to show any response. This time, when she looked back at me,

I made a funny face and stuck out my tongue, then smelled my left armpit and made another face.

And finally—*finally*—I got her to crack a smile.

Sitting on the bench at courtside, I watched them warm up. Kim's strokes were mechanical and uninspired. Ginny still had a languidness about her. I turned and looked at the bleachers, which were jammed full. Halfway up I spotted Donsprokken and Dirk and Bitsy, all three sitting together and hiding behind sunglasses. Each in turn nodded or waved at me, and I nodded back and could feel their eyes still on me after I had turned away.

Ginny came over to the bench and shed her sweats and took a sip of high-tech liquid.

"I have to go now," I said. The linesmen were taking their seats in their folding metal chairs and the umpire was about to sit in the tall lifeguard chair above the net. "You need anything? A pep talk?"

"Luck."

"Play your heart out," I told her. I took her hand and squeezed it.

She leaned toward me and planted a not-so-quick kiss on my mouth. Her lips were cool and pillowy and salty, softer than I could ever have imagined.

"That's for luck," she said.

20

I GOT UP from the bench and walked off the court, keeping my eyes down to avoid having to look at the dozens of people, including Ginny's parents and Donsprokken, who had seen the kiss. I had to get out of there. I had to think.

Strangely enough, I was empty-handed. I had left Ginny's tennis bag and the cooler at courtside for Ginny to use and I'd left my tennis racket locked in the Jeep under the driver's seat. I'd used a towel to reserve my spot in the first row of the bleachers. I walked away from it all, the whole area, past the tennis courts with their matches in progress, through a gate, up the wooded trail into a portion of the same park where Ginny had played her qualifying match on the satellite court the day before yesterday.

I could still taste the kiss. There was something

defeated and resigned about it. Ginny was going to lose today. Was it just a feeling I had, or something more than that? Was it a wish? Did I want Ginny to lose?

Maybe if she fell on her face against Korticek, she'd come home for good. "Nobody wants to be friends with a loser," went the Stan Claxton pep talk. Except of course another loser.

I kept walking, farther up the wooded hillside. Ginny would be looking for me, wondering where I'd gone, thinking I'd deserted her. I couldn't sit there and watch her lose. I didn't want to be around Donsprokken. I had to admit, the thought of him and Ginny all over each other was painful.

Time passed. I found a viewpoint overlooking the twelve courts below. I could just make out the yellow tennis balls in play. I could see Ginny and Kim. I could see the scoreboard, too, the individual numbers hanging on the chain-link fence and updated after each game by the nearest linesman. I squinted so I could read the numbers:

	1	2	3
G. Forrester	2		
K. Korticek	5		

They slugged it out from the baseline, long rallies, neither of them going to the net. Each game, the linesman put up a new number. Kim Korticek won the first set, 6–2. Right away, she broke Ginny's serve in the second. She led 2–0, then 3–1. My heart felt sick.

During the change of sides they sat on their respective benches. I could almost see the sweat glistening on Ginny's legs, stretched out in front of her. She wiped her arms and face and neck with a towel. She didn't look like she had given up. She had never given up before. I had given up for her, but what did that matter? What did she have left now? Whatever she had was something inside her, something I didn't know. Had I ever known it? I tried to think back to some time in my life I could be proud of, but nothing came. I had done it all half-assed. No wonder I stole nickels and dimes and books and tennis rackets. What did I have that was mine, inside me? I didn't even have honor.

I knew there was no way I could ever want her to fall on her face. But what did that matter? I also knew there was no way I'd ever set foot in Donsprokken's tennis camp. I'd had a feeling there was something false about his offer from the start.

I drifted along the trail. It led over a knoll, out of view of the tennis courts. There was no one up here, no one. The trail went past the satellite court where Ginny and Antonia had played. No one was using it now. The trail circled around, and pretty soon I found myself back at the viewpoint of the twelve courts. Ginny and Kim were still playing. Ginny had hung on—was hanging on. She was now down only 3–4 in the second set.

I sat on the dirt path to rest. I was hot and sweaty and thirsty. Their rallies seemed endless. Each point was an individual battle with its own intricate pattern, its own series of moves, like a chess match. Ginny was winning more points now. They kept working from the baseline, trying to maneuver each other out of position for the kill. Every time the point ended, the crowd exploded into applause and cheers. They were making shots they hadn't made earlier. Hardly any errors; winning the points by sheer craft. It was strange, but there were moments during the long rallies that I forgot who was who, Ginny and Kim seemed to be identical. The crowd was cheering for both of them. I could feel it way up where I sat. They both had it. I had it, too, all the way up here. "Like something flowing through you . . . You can't will it to happen." The gift, free and unearned.

"What the hell happened to you?" Donsprokken said.

Donsprokken, Dirk, and Bitsy were standing beside Ginny at courtside. The match had been over for twenty minutes. The crowd had thinned. Two new players were getting ready to warm up. Ginny looked sweaty and radiant. She gave me a flicker of a smile, and I smiled back. Dirk and Bitsy wanted to drive her home. As she passed by me, her hand brushed against my arm.

"You and I need to talk," Donsprokken said. He told me to come with him. We traipsed off to a remote corner of a nearby soccer field, where there were no witnesses. He kept his sunglasses on while he yelled at me.

"You dumb twit," he said. "You only missed the greatest third set of all time." He poked his index finger in my chest. "A coach, mister, does not give up on his player. You wrote her off, that's what you did. You wrote her off. You gave up on her. Admit it, man. Shame on you."

I didn't say anything. I couldn't look at him. I wasn't afraid, but I saw my own reflection in his sunglasses.

"Up until today," he went on, now pointing at the ground instead of my chest and talking in an almost singsong cadence, "I'll have to admit you've done a fairly decent job of coaching Ginny in this tournament. I suppose you've helped her. But you blew it today, and no matter what she says, Claxton, you need to be a man and step down as her coach for the rest of this tournament and let me take over."

"Nope," I said.

"Nope? You don't have any right. You don't deserve it. You walked out on her. Give me one reason why you should be her coach."

"She wants me."

"She doesn't know what she wants. Look, man, I'll make it easy for you. You step down as her coach or I'll take back my generous offer and you can kiss my tennis camp goodbye."

"I already have," I said.

"Already have what?"

"Kissed it goodbye."

Donsprokken took a breath, then smiled. He was using his tongue to probe for something stuck between his rear molars. "Ah. Well, then. She's talked to you. I knew she would. You two are such little girlfriends."

"That's why you offered me the tennis camp, right out of the blue. You thought I'd be on your side or something."

"All you've heard is her side. How about hearing mine?"

"No."

"Why not? You afraid of what you'll hear?"

"Yes."

Donsprokken stopped smiling. "Just understand one thing, Stan. If you—if you plan on making trouble for me, it's Ginny you'll be screwing, not me. It's her life. Ginny and I have worked this out. It's done and settled and forgotten. I want you to know that. Any problems you make, you'll only hurt *her*."

———

That night Ginny called me. I told her what Donsprokken had said. I told her I'd step aside and let
Donsprokken take over if she wanted me to. She said
she didn't. Then she said, "How come you didn't tell
him you were up there, dummy?"

"What?"

"I saw you watching me from those trees. Way up
there. I almost waved at you, but I figured maybe you
didn't want anyone to know you were up there. And
a player's not allowed to wave at her coach during a
match anyway, even if he's a few thousand feet away.
But just knowing you were up there watching me, it
made a difference."

"Oh come on."

"Really," she said. "It did."

"There was *some* difference all right. It wasn't me,
but it was something."

"Kim felt it, too," she said. "Kim told me right after
the match, she played her heart out. She wasn't disappointed. She said it's the first time she's ever lost
and not felt like a loser. It's what I've been looking
for for a long time. I don't know why it chose today,
or why it waited till the third set, but it sure came.
It's why I came home in the first place. At least one
reason why. You're a reason, too. Maybe the main reason. I knew you wouldn't walk out on me."

"I almost did."

"Why?"

"Because it hurts to watch you."

"Why?"

"Because in a few days this'll all be over. Just like the snow day and that hike up to Barrow Falls and everything else. You're on your way. Nothing's going to stop you and nothing should stop you. And I shouldn't be sad about that. I am, but I shouldn't be."

The next day, Saturday, Ginny beat the flashy Tiger Yamashita—or "Tiger the Immaculate," as she was called—in the semis, 4–6, 7–6, 6–1. On Sunday at noon, in the finals, she lost in three sets, all tiebreakers, to the eighteen-year-old number-two player from USC. That evening was the awards banquet, which I didn't attend, and after that, a party thrown by Dirk and Bitsy, which I did attend. The guests included some sponsors and financial backers, my parents, and Donsprokken—and Guballa and Wilcutts, who behaved themselves and didn't break anything and only offended two or three people. I stayed till the end, till everyone had left, and Ginny and I stood out on the deck with Boat between us.

"I forgot to tell you about a phone call I got," she said. "You'll never guess who from."

"Let's see . . . Yoko?"

"No."

"Antonia Wheeler?"

"No. No, the president of Randall Swordfight Cat

Food. He's going to send me a special-delivery package. A video that shows their factory and how they put only top-quality ingredients into their cat food, and five coupons for free cat food. The president said Boat was probably just mad at me for being gone so long."

"Him and me both," I said. We were silent for a minute.

"Donsprokken told me you turned down the tennis camp," she said. "Aren't you kind of shooting yourself in the foot?"

"Yeah, but I guess I'm stuck with my runts. They need me."

"So do I. What was that thing you wanted to tell me? Remember? You were going to tell me something."

"When are you leaving?" I asked.

She looked surprised. "How did you know? I only found out an hour ago."

"Well, I'd say it was inevitable."

"Day after tomorrow," she said.

"That soon?"

"He—we—Team Donsprokken—there's a national tournament in Chicago we need to gear up for. Then down South to the academy. Then up North for a couple of biggies. Then we're going to Europe. The whole year's planned out."

"I'd have to say I'm a little jealous," I said. "I mean, of all that traveling."

"Then you think I should go?"

I drew in my breath and looked at her. "Are you kidding?"

"No. I'm considering."

"Considering what?"

"Staying here."

"What would you do?"

She shrugged. "Go to school. Play tennis. Do homework. Join the French club. Eat fast food. Go on dates."

Something was rising in my chest. Elation. It almost made me yell out, but I willed it down. "Did you tell Donsprokken? Your parents? That you have doubts?"

"Well, there wasn't time. They just gave me the whole plan right in the middle of the party. I didn't say anything at all. I'm just—I'm still debating."

"You don't have much time to debate," I said.

"No. Tomorrow I have to pack. Tomorrow night would be our last night—"

"Whose?"

"Yours and mine—I mean, if I were to go. If I didn't go, it wouldn't be. Of course."

"The ballet's tomorrow night, you know," I said.

"That's right! You want to go?"

"Do you?"

"We'd have to get dressed up. Can you borrow a suit and tie from Wilcutts's great-grandfather?"

"Yeah. How about you? Can you borrow a dress?"

"I don't have to borrow a dress, dummy. But what if we get all dressed up and go there and it turns out there aren't any tickets waiting for us at the window?"

"Ginny," I said, "there won't be any tickets waiting for us."

"Oh."

"In which case," I said, "we'll have to wing it."

"We're good at that," she said.

21

SO IT WAS OUR LAST NIGHT together.
Maybe.

I borrowed a suit and tie and shoes from Wilcutts's great-grandfather. My own father owned a couple of outrageous sport jackets but not a single suit,
and the three or four times in his life he'd had to wear
a formal suit, he'd borrowed it from Wilcutts's great-
grandfather. Wilcutts's great-grandfather was "no
longer with us"; he had departed this life eleven years
ago, leaving behind an entire bedroom full of memo-
rabilia, a veritable museum that paid homage to the
fourteen years he had lived with the Wilcuttses. His
walk-in closet contained at least a dozen suits and evening jackets of different shades, with a rack of assorted
ties. The suit I chose was a gray flannel with enormous
square padded shoulders and pants so baggy they

212

flapped. The brown shoes were comfortable but a bit too big; they were the kind with holes in the sides of them, like old Buicks.

From my room, I heard Ginny's voice downstairs. She had finished dressing and had come over to my house so that we could get an early start. I descended the stairs like a debutante on prom night. She was sitting on the couch talking to my parents, and when she saw me, she whistled. I whistled back. She wore a slinky black dress held up by two thin straps. Your basic Tainted Woman dress.

My mother made us stand on the front porch so she could take our picture. Dad handed me some money and the keys to his Tercel and cautioned me about the wiper blades.

As we were getting into the car, Dirk and Bitsy came walking up the driveway. Dirk was carrying his video camera. Our parents were going out to dinner later.

"Have her home by her twenty-first birthday, Stan," Dirk said.

"Aren't they a handsome couple?" Bitsy said. Everyone agreed. We had to go back to the front porch and start over, so Dirk could shoot some video of us walking to the car. This time, still on camera, I opened Ginny's door for her. I got in, started the car, and backed cautiously down the driveway. The neighbors came out to see what was going on.

"What a send-off," I said.

"Everyone's in a good mood," she said.

"Old Ginny's back on track," I said.

"It's easy to make people happy," she said. "You just do what they want you to do."

"Are you doing that?"

She didn't answer for a few seconds. Then said half-seriously, "I'm waiting for a sign. A bolt of lightning or something."

Lightning did come. During the ride to the Seattle Opera House southbound on I–5, there was thunder, lightning, pouring rain, the whole works. Four lanes of traffic stood at a dead halt. Sirens wailed behind us: police cars, fire trucks, and aid units edged by on the left shoulder.

"Nothing like a highway fatality to start off the evening," I said.

"Stop that," she said.

We had not moved for several minutes.

"Wouldn't it be weird if we spent the whole evening stuck right here?" she said.

"That would be special," I said.

"I have to keep reminding myself I shouldn't have high expectations about tonight," she said.

"What a sweet way to put it," I said.

"I didn't mean . . ." She smiled weakly.

The four lanes of traffic were being diverted into the far right lane. We crawled past wrecked cars pointed every which way, and flashing red, yellow, and blue lights. I started to say something about signs and omens but kept my mouth shut.

We parked in the multi-level garage and took the overpass to the Opera House. Rain slanted down, but we stayed dry all the way to the entrance of the Opera House. It had been designed that way. You could walk from car to opera without being touched by a drop of rain. What a world.

All kinds of people were milling around in front of the Opera House. People in evening clothes, jewels, furs; people carrying signs protesting the wearing of dead animals; cops everywhere; limos pulling up to disgorge groups of white-haired people.

There was no line at the Will Call window. A girl nineteen or twenty, wearing red lipstick and a red uniform reminiscent of *Star Trek*, greeted us.

"My name is on a list," I told her.

"I bet your name's on a lot of lists," she said.

"This is a list of people who've been left tickets by somebody who knows somebody who's in the ballet or something like that. I'm not exactly sure."

"*That* list? You're on *that* list?"

"I wouldn't bet the farm on it."

I told her my name. Spelled it. She flipped through a box of index cards. "Hm. Nope. No Claxton here."

"Why am I not surprised," I said.

"Here's a *Clap*ton," she said. "And in parentheses

it says tennis mister. Or is that meister. And it says A. Wheeler. You a tennismeister?"

"Mister or master, loosely speaking."

"Good enough for me. Here you go." She handed me four tickets.

"Whoa," I said. "Four? We only need two."

"Congratulations," the girl said. "You have now found yourself in the enviable position of having two extra tickets."

Ginny and I both thanked her and turned from the window. "By Jove," I said, "I'm going to scalp these puppies. Donate the money to my favorite charity."

"The Claxton Foundation?" Ginny said.

"Built on sand," I said.

A crowd of desperate-looking people watched me approach them, as if wondering but not quite believing I could have tickets. We moved on down the wall. My heart was beating in a frenzy.

I spotted a short man standing with a girl of about nine or ten who was unquestionably his daughter. The girl wore her hair pulled back in a ballerina's bun. The short man had glasses and muttonchop whiskers and a bald head and a nice face, kind of scrunched-up and funny-looking. Here was the one-in-a-hundred guy who'd pull over on the deserted highway and help you with your flat tire.

"Are you looking for tickets?" I asked.

"Yeah! Are the seats together?" He pulled out his wallet and dug into it. "Name your price."

"Take 'em."

"What?" He was pulling twenties from his wallet. His hands were trembling. "Please," he said. "Hey, come on, it's immoral to give those tickets away. Downright immoral. At least let me pay what they're worth."

"I didn't pay anything for them," I said.

He stood shaking his head. "You're a . . . you're a good man."

I rejoined Ginny, who'd been standing a few feet away, watching.

"Ready to go inside," I said, "or you want to hang around this circus and—"

She reached up and kissed me on the cheek. "My contribution to the Claxton Foundation," she said.

Our seats were on the second floor, in what is called the loge section on the mezzanine level. Where you could lean over the railing and look down women's dresses.

"Mezzanine," Ginny said. "That's a pretty word, isn't it?"

"Right up there with peacock," I said.

The seats were in a private box. The box was at one end of the horseshoe, right over the stage. It had eight red velvet chairs, four front, four back. Our seats were in the front, next to the wall. Behind us sat two old couples. The women were very elegant, big silver-haired ladies with jewels. One of them was fat, the other skinny and birdlike.

Leaning toward me, Ginny said, "Look at all those old people down there. I bet they all ate before they came here."

"So?"

"So they're all sitting there digesting their meals."

"Oh," I said. "Yeah." Then I said, "I wonder if we're supposed to introduce ourselves to our box-mates. Since we're sharing a box and all."

"It might be the civil thing to do."

The place was filling up with more old people digesting their meals. The two seats next to us, which I'd given to that short guy and his daughter, were still empty. My right leg bounced uncontrollably. I was pretty excited. Ginny leaned forward and started to take off her sweater, and I thought that the gallant thing to do would be to assist, but then I thought, Hell, she ain't crippled. But then I thought I'd better do it anyway, just to appear chivalrous to the people behind us, but by the time I turned to her, one of the old gentlemen behind her was sliding the white cashmere off her thin-strapped shoulders, getting an eyeful of clear, tanned skin. Ginny turned around, blushing, her teeth looking whiter than I'd ever seen them. "Thank you!"

"My pleasure," the man said, bowing slightly.

I turned and cleared my throat. "I would have done it myself except I was momentarily paralyzed."

The man smiled and nodded.

"What a lovely dress," the birdlike woman said.

Ginny blushed again and nodded in thanks.

I cleared my throat again. "I guess since we're box-mates, I should introduce us. I'm Stan Claxton and this is Ginny Forrester."

They said how do you do and introduced themselves.

"Your skin is so lovely," the fat woman warbled. "Have you been to the Caribbean, perhaps?"

"Why, yes," Ginny said, blushing.

"I think she means recently," I said. "Not when you were in the sixth grade."

"You shertainly have exsheptional sheats," the bearded man said. His name was John Hognash. His mouth was full of green pellets. His wife had been feeding him Tic Tacs.

The other man's name was LeRoy Blankenship. I noticed that his name was listed on the program as being a Gold Member. I wondered if, when he was a kid, the other kids had called him Blankety-Blank. I believe I would have.

Blankety-Blank's wife said to me, "Claxton. Claxton. You're not related to Mrs. Homer Guptill Claxton, are you?"

"I don't think I'd want to be related to a lady named Homer," I said.

The lights flashed and dimmed, meaning, sit down and shut up. A minute later, the curtain of our box parted and in walked two people.

Not the short guy and his daughter. Instead, they were a tall couple, a man with a well-groomed beard and a woman with gray-streaked hair. I would have guessed they were the owners of an art gallery or maybe a poodle-grooming parlor.

They looked at Ginny and me, then at their tickets, then at the empty seats, then at each other, and sat down.

"I don't believe it," I muttered to Ginny. "I do not hoppin' believe it."

"Don't believe what?"

"He scalped 'em. The short guy and his daughter. They scalped the tickets."

"No! That nice man? He was so sweet."

"They're probably tossing down vodka-and-tonics at the corner bar this very minute. Or heading for the shopping mall."

"I hope they buy a lot of crap they don't need," Ginny said.

"I just wonder how much they got for 'em."

"Ask."

"That would probably be considered tacky," I said.

"Look, there's Antonia!" Ginny said. "Hey, look, she's waving up here."

There she was, wearing her hair in an elegant swirl atop her head and a green, summery, formal gown, sitting next to a tall man with slumped shoulders and short gray hair and sunglasses. I waved back.

"Thank you!" Ginny said. Whether Antonia heard her or simply read her lips, she understood, and made a thumbs-up.

"I'm sorry we ever doubted her," Ginny said.

I felt a tap on my left shoulder.

"Pardon me," Blankety-Blank said. "The young lady you just waved to. We couldn't help speculating on whether the man sitting next to her might possibly be Clint Eastwood."

I smiled. "You know, I have to believe it is."

Midway through the first act I glanced at Ginny to see how she was enjoying the ballet. She was leaning forward in her seat, her lips parted, eyes wide, her whole self motionless. There was a rapt, faraway look on her face, as if she were listening to a one-legged sailor telling her the story of how his leg had got chomped off. For a moment, I almost wanted to cry. My heart swelled with some nameless emotion.

When the ballet ended there was a standing ovation. Ginny and I stood and ovated with everyone else.

I took a deep breath and turned to the bearded man next to me.

"Sir, do you mind if I ask you a tacky question?"

"You can ask it. I don't know if I'll answer it."

"Did you buy your tickets from a short guy with muttonchop whiskers?"

"Yes, I did."

"Do you mind my asking what you paid for them?"

The man fingered his beard. He obviously didn't know whether or not it was beneath his dignity to answer the question. I sensed that he spent a lot of time deciding whether something was beneath his dignity or not. After a long pause, he said, "Five and a quarter for the pair."

I nodded and sat down. The theater swirled. For a few seconds I couldn't breathe.

Ginny and I stayed seated until the place had emptied. Finally, we got up and made our way to the lobby.

I said, "That's the closest I've ever come to fainting. I'm going to duck into the rest room."

"Remember now," Ginny said, "it was only money. I'll wait out here."

In the rest room there was one other man, a distinguished-looking white-haired gentleman. He didn't see me. He was looking at himself in the mirror. Or rather, leaning over the sink, not looking at himself but peering beyond his reflection, into some other dimension. He was saying, "Hello! Hello? Hello?"

I turned around and walked out.

"What's wrong?" Ginny asked.

"God! Come on, let's get out of this place." I took

her arm and we headed down the stairs toward the exit doors.

I let go of her arm, and she linked it through mine. "What's the matter?" she asked. "What happened back there?"

"There was a man in there," I said. "He looked like the CEO of IBM or something. He was sort of gazing at himself in the mirror or, rather, *beyond* himself, beyond his image, saying, 'Hello! Hello?' "

"Oh," Ginny said, "he was probably trying to connect with his Little Child Within. I think that's one way you're supposed to do it."

"You know all the tricks, don't you," I said. "You and Dr. Teresa Ponti. I just don't understand why he had to do it in a public rest room."

"Well, you're supposed to do it after you've been moved emotionally. The ballet probably affected him so profoundly that he had to run off in search of his LCW right away, while it was still near the surface."

"Yeah, but in a public rest room. People ought to be more considerate."

"Now, now, Coach, don't let it bother you."

It was time to set the next leg of my plan into motion. We got in the car and drove twenty or so miles north to a place that I called the Titan Site. I wasn't sure what its official name was; as far as I knew, it wasn't even on a map. It was on a high hill overlooking the north end of Lake Washington. At the top of the hill was a large fenced-in area, similar to a reservoir, only it was just a grassy field. There were no street-lights and it was very dark. The rain had stopped and the night sky had cleared. I pulled into the parking lot of a little park; just a strip of a no-name park, with one lone picnic table. Beyond the mowed grass was tall weeds, and then trees, but tonight you could not see the picnic table or grass or trees or anything else.

"What's this place, Stan?" Ginny whispered.

"Used to be a Titan missile site," I said. "Missiles are—or were—buried right in the ground and pointed at—at whatever they used to point them at. The tips of those Titan missiles are made out of the same material as—"

"As your tennis racket?"

"You got it."

"Are the missiles deactivated or whatever?"

"You're asking the wrong guy."

She paused. "This sure is a secluded spot. Is this what you wanted to show me?"

"No." I took a deep breath, let it out, and turned off the headlights. "I wanted to show you *this*."

22

"IT'S AWFULLY CREEPY," Ginny whispered.

"Shhh. You have to be very quiet. Keep looking straight ahead."

"Wh-what am I looking for?"

"You'll see."

For about two minutes we sat looking out at the darkness.

"Is this a joke? I don't see anything."

"Shh!"

There it was. I tapped her on the shoulder and pointed slightly to the right. "Look."

She drew in a breath. "Oh! I see it! What is it?"

Two eyes glowed from the darkness. They stayed there, alive and burning.

"Is it an animal?" she asked.

"I don't know. Maybe a cat or raccoon or some other varmint. It's been there, doing that, since March. Guballa and Wilcutts and I discovered it one night."

"It really is spooky. I've seen cat's eyes glow like that."

"They'll go away in a minute or two."

They did.

Ginny turned to me. "You know something? You're interesting just about all the time."

"Yeah?"

We were quiet for a while.

Pretty soon Ginny sighed. "I suppose this is one of those places where people park and make out."

"I'll be right back," I said.

"Where are you going? Oh. Don't get bitten by anything. I'll stay here and look for shooting stars."

"You'd better lock your door. And lock mine, too."

"Don't be silly. You're trying to frighten me. Just leave your keys here in case you get eaten or something."

I left my keys in the ignition and got out and plunged into the darkness. I could not guarantee that there were no holes or ditches or swamps that I might fall into, it was that dark, the kind of dark where your eyes go cross-eyed because they can't focus on anything. Somewhere out in the middle of the field, underneath the starry sky, I unzipped my fly and made my offering to Mother Earth.

I felt exposed and vulnerable out there in the dark. I was getting that old Belgian-waffle feeling.

I looked up at the swirl of stars. I saw a shooting star, then another. Two golf balls, incredibly bright, streaking across the sky. Meteoric. I thought of Ginny waiting back in the car. Suddenly, for no apparent reason, a wave of joy hit me with a rush and a shiver. It was the kind of feeling you get when you crawl between fresh cold sheets on a winter night, or when you have a good sneeze, or when you wake up in the morning and find that it has snowed all night and school has been canceled.

There was one thing you could say about life: it hurled crap at you, but there were windows of joy. There were people who pinched you or looked into the mirror for their LCW; people who scalped free ballet tickets; took advantage; grabbed whatever gift came their way, no matter whether it was right or wrong, and then rationalized it. There were people like Antonia Wheeler, who stole tennis rackets and songs, but just when you thought you had them pegged, they surprised you.

There were people like Wilcutts and Guballa, who were so predictable that they never surprised you; they told stories about junior high days and would not forget certain things that had happened to them, like girls being on their soccer team or a dumb kiss. But somehow you knew you'd always be able to count on them.

And there were the losers. So many losers, like my runts. But what made somebody a loser? By whose standards? Those runts would never be beautiful people, but I loved them. They were my team.

There were people like Ginny, who grew beyond you, and left. But they left you *with* something. A gift, free and clear.

I went back to the car. As I had expected, Ginny had locked all the doors. She leaned over and unlocked my side.

"Here you go." She handed me a packet of her moist towelettes.

"I knew I could count on you," I said. I wiped my hands with the lemon-scented towelette. "Wow, you know something, Ginny? I had a sort of experience out there. I won't call it a religious experience, but—"

"Why not?" Ginny asked.

"Huh?"

"Why won't you call it a religious experience?"

"Because I was urinating. You don't have religious experiences while urinating. But let me tell you what happened. I was looking up at the sky, at the stars, and I saw two shooting stars—"

"Hey, I think I saw the same ones," Ginny said.

"Really? I had a feeling. Anyway, I felt this—this well-being. I don't know if it was God or what. But I really felt it."

"What did it feel like?" she asked.

"Oh, a lot of things. Like clarity and—and intensity, like when you're in the middle of a tennis match against a great opponent. Like sometimes when you and I would play a match, I'd feel that way. Ginny, I've been an idiot."

"Why?"

"Because I've been waiting. I keep waiting for things to happen. You know that thing I was going to tell you? Well, I've been waiting for the right time. As if there's such a thing as a 'right' time. That's crazy. You either do something or you don't do it. This is going to be hard for me to put into words; I've never told anybody. Not another living soul. One reason I haven't told anybody is that I've been waiting for the 'right' person or 'special' person or whatever. The other reason is, well, I guess what I've really been afraid of is how that special person I tell would *react*. Does that make sense? It's not that I'm afraid of what they'll think of *me*—that I'm nuts or a fool or a liar. It's that I'm afraid of what I'll think about *them*, if I tell them and they don't—they don't react right. They'd lose their specialness. If I tell somebody I really respect and they react *wrong*, then I'd lose respect for them."

"So it's like a test," Ginny said.

"In a way, yeah, a test."

"You're afraid to give the test to someone, because you don't want to see them fail."

"Exactly."

"Have you picked me?"

"Yes."

"But you've tipped me off. That's not a fair test. You've given me an advantage. You didn't give me a chance to pass on my own."

"That's true," I said, thinking. "All right, how about if you pretend I didn't tip you off. You react exactly how you would have reacted if I hadn't warned you it was a test. Can you do that without cheating?"

She gave it some thought. "Yes."

"All right. Okay. There are these toilets."

She rolled her eyes. "Oh, Stan!"

"No, no, listen. Come on now. They defy description. But I'll do my best. Think of trying to describe how you felt during the first act of that ballet. Kind of rapt and awed. Well, that's what I'm going to try to describe to you. There are four of them. Four toilets. They're at the Brothers of Kfordne Brotherhood Lodge."

"The place where you used to clean toilets?"

"Right. Remember, I used to scrub the toilets on Sunday night, when nobody else was there."

"That's the best time to scrub them," Ginny said. "While no one else is using them."

"Two-point deduction on the test for making a dumb joke."

"Sorry. Go on."

"You're good at visualizations, so picture this. Four toilets, all in a row. No walls, no stalls, no partitions."

"You're kidding."

"No."

"Like four men are going to sit there using them all at the same time? I don't think so."

I nodded. "You've got the picture. So anyway, when—"

"Stan, why don't they have *stalls*?"

"Ginny, I don't know. Those Brothers of Kfordne are pretty tight with the purse strings, you know. It costs money to put up stalls. Now listen, are you going to let me tell you this?"

"No."

"No?"

"I want you to show me. I mean, you said they defy description. So why even try? Let me see them for myself. If it's a test you want to give me, then give me the real thing. That'll be the *real* test."

I stared at her. I swallowed. She had me. Once again, she had me.

I hesitated, then reached for the ignition and started the car, and we took off for the Brothers of Kfordne Lodge.

23

TWENTY MINUTES LATER, we climbed
into the lodge through the rear window with the
busted latch that the Brothers of Kfordne had never
gotten around to fixing. We groped our way through
darkness to the bathroom, where it was safe enough
to flip on the lights, illuminating two sinks, one long
rectangular mirror, one aftershave lotion dispenser,
one paper towel dispenser.

And the four toilets, side by side. Black U-shaped
seats on white bowls. Chrome flush handles.

There was always the possibility that it wouldn't
work this time, or that a plumber had done some hoo-
doo on them. But they had never *not* worked. Still,
my hands were trembling and my palms were sweaty.

Outside, a car approached and seemed to slow

down. Its brakes squeaked, gravel crunched. Then the car sped up again. Probably made a U-turn.

"Should we turn off the lights?" Ginny whispered.

I nodded. I reached out and flipped the switch. The bathroom went dark, but our eyes adjusted to the grades of light. Ginny's eyes were luminous.

"Anything I should do?" she asked, looking at me.

"No. Yes. This is important. You have to wait. That sounds obvious, but you'll be tempted to—well, listen, I have to flush all four, one right after the other, and when I do, it's going to be pretty loud. We're talking industrial-strength flush. Then it'll get quieter, and then absolute silence. That silence lasts about, oh, fifteen or twenty seconds, and that length of time, it seems like forever, it really does. So you have to wait it out. Don't make me shush you. Got that?"

"Got it."

"Okay." I rubbed my hands together, feeling my breath quicken. "Okay."

I showed Ginny where to stand, where the acoustics were best. She leaned against the sink in her slinky black dress with its two thin straps, facing the toilets.

I gripped the first handle. It was cool and moist and metallic in my warm palm. I closed my eyes for a second and then flushed. Not hurrying, I stepped to the second one and flushed. Plenty of time. Don't hurry. Number three, ready, grip, flush. Then the fourth. Then I went over and stood next to Ginny.

The roaring, gushing, slurping was deafening. A tremendous whooshing sound came as water surged into the tanks. Then a long hiss that lasted about ten seconds. The hiss grew fainter, fainter, then fell silent.

Silence.

Nothing to do now but wait. We waited. I prayed that a loud truck or motorcycle wouldn't go by outside. But there were no sounds from the road; it was deserted.

Had I said fifteen seconds of silence? It seemed more like fifteen minutes. Ginny, beside me, was perfectly still, except maybe for her breathing, and her eyes.

Finally, the first sound came. A low, flat whistle. Was it the pipes or something else? I'd never been able to figure it out. Then another toilet joined in shrilly, then another in a different key. All four whistled separately, yet their notes seemed to interact. The music rose and quavered in melodious, eerie, haunting trills. It sounded like high-pitched flutes and recorders. Or like those underwater recordings of whales—whalesong. Or like Bing Crosby when he whistles in the middle of "White Christmas." It grew louder, a crescendo, reaching its highest and loudest intensity. Ginny's eyes were wide.

Then, in its third minute, the song softly subsided and fell silent.

Ginny took my hand and held it against her cheek. I felt how hot her cheek was. Her eyes were moist, fixed on mine. All I had to do was say it now. Say it: *Don't go. Stay here forever.*

But the next thing I knew we were kissing, a "prolonged series" of them, and there wasn't time to talk.

I suppose I could have said something to her while we were driving home. We hardly spoke. I could have brought it up then, asked her to stay. We could have had a big discussion about it.

Or I could have said it the next day, while we stood facing each other in the sunlight in her driveway, holding each other's hands. While her parents sat waiting in the Jeep Cherokee with the engine running, to drive her to the airport.

"Thanks for everything, Coach," she said, looking into my eyes. "Especially for last night. I'll never tell anybody about—I swear, I'll never tell anyone."

I smiled. "Not even your future husband twenty years from now?"

"Oh, him! God, he'll be disgusted if I tell him. He'll roll his eyes and say, 'Now, really, dear, what nonsense. Whistling toilets? How vulgar.' And I'll think, Geesh! I married this guy? Or I'll be sitting around the table with his parents—my in-laws—who will be very snobby, of course, and the subject of Bing Crosby will come up, and I'll say, 'Oh, speaking of Bing Crosby, did you know there are these toilets . . .'"

I laughed. We both did. Part of me was only pretending to laugh, because if I didn't keep busy laugh-

ing I'd probably break down in the driveway. I gave
her a quick final hug and we said goodbye.

And I returned to Sour Lake, with its cracked
courts and sagging nets and the ShopRite shopping
cart full of tennis balls, and the aerobics instructor,
and the runts, always the runts. I was never more glad
to be anywhere. Over the next few weeks I lined up
several tennis matches for my team against neighbor-
ing rec centers and club teams, and my team was not
really much worse or more embarrassing than the
teams from Ballard or Rainier Beach or Laurelhurst
or Madrona. We won some and lost some, and no one
seemed to mind either way.

And the Boxton racket? the joy of my life? I kept
using it. But as Ginny had so accurately put it, my
conscience occasionally jumped up and bit me. No
doubt to remind me that it, my conscience, was still
hanging on. I couldn't shake either one of them—my
conscience or the racket. Maybe someday another Antonia Wheeler would come along and steal it from me.
Or I'd sell it. Or give it away to the "right" person:
some deserving runt—who then might just as likely
turn around and sell it to the highest bidder, as that
muttonchopped man had done with the ballet tickets
I'd given him. Who could tell what anyone would do
or who the "right" person was? My right person had
been living a few hundred feet away from me my
whole life.

———

One night in early August, my parents came home from an evening out with Dirk and Bitsy, and my mother tapped on my door and stuck her head in and announced that she had some shocking news: Ginny had dumped Donsprokken, moved to a new tennis academy in Sarasota, Florida, and hired a new personal coach. Dirk and Bitsy were flabbergasted. I wasn't.

School started. I shifted my Sour Lake hours back to part-time. A new crop of runts. I bought an old Ford Escort from an ad in the classifieds, and Guballa showed me how to change the oil. I still hung out with Guballa and Wilcutts, though I'd be damned if I'd come up with a "signature honk."

I spent a lot of time walking, kicking piles of fallen leaves, watching the rain.

I didn't go back to the Whistling Toilets. Maybe I never would—not without Ginny. One evening I telephoned the Brothers of Kfordne during their lodge meeting and told them, in a disguised voice, that if they didn't fix their busted back window, I was going to crawl in one night and ransack their lodge and steal all their ceremonial hats.

I did go back to the satellite court where Ginny and I had waited for Antonia Wheeler to arrive. It hadn't changed. The broken beer bottles and debris had come back, and the net still sagged. I stood looking at the brown leaves strewn across the court. The rain gently tapped on them. I remembered the

scratching sound of the push broom as I had swept
the debris.

I reread my two Arthur Ashe books. When I finished *Advantage Ashe*, I took it back to my old school
library. As I turned away empty-handed from the return slot, I couldn't quite believe what I'd just done.

Toward the end of the third week of school I got
a letter from Ginny. It was a typical letter of hers,
rather disjointed, mostly news and information, excited and upbeat. She told me about her bold move
and about her new coach and new tennis academy. It
was the same academy that Kim Korticek went to. In
fact, she and Kim had become friends.

In the last paragraph Ginny mentioned that there
was going to be a tournament up in Vancouver, B.C.
My heart rose and I immediately began plotting how
I could drive up there and meet her for a day or even
an hour. But I read further. Ginny was getting ready
for a tournament in South Carolina. The tournament
in Vancouver was a men's pro tournament. I was puzzled. Why would she tell me about . . . ?

Then it clicked.

24

ON THE FIRST THURSDAY in October I skipped school, with my parents' permission, and drove my Ford Escort three hours to a tennis club in Vancouver, B.C. I found Gerald Boxton's first-round match and watched him get eliminated by a Frenchman named Merot, 6–3, 7–5.

Afterward, I sat in my car in a remote corner of the club parking lot, staking out the front doors of the clubhouse. A limo pulled up, and a minute later Gerald Boxton emerged from the clubhouse alone, carrying an athletic bag, and climbed into the limo. I followed the limo to an opulent hotel in downtown Vancouver. Boxton got out and strode past the doorman into the hotel. I wasn't far behind him, having parked illegally in the loading zone. The doorman smiled and nodded to me. I saw Boxton go up a flight of royally carpeted stairs and into the hotel cocktail lounge.

I knew the drinking age in Canada was eighteen. I was a few months shy of seventeen, but I figured no one would ask me for ID as long as I didn't try to order a drink, which I had no intention of doing.

Boxton sat by himself at a round table in a dark corner and ordered a drink from the cocktail waitress. He unzipped his athletic bag and took out a pair of brown slippers. They looked comfortable and expensive. The skin of some animal, no doubt. He removed the shoes he was wearing, put on the slippers, stuck the street shoes into the bag, zipped it back up, and settled in to wait for his drink. I went back out to my Ford Escort and found a legal parking spot two blocks away. I grabbed the tennis racket from the back seat.

When I returned to the lounge, his lordship was sipping a Bloody Mary, staring at nothing in particular. I approached him.

"Lord Boxton?"

He glanced up at me. His eyes were quick and fierce, beady and bloodshot. "What."

"Could I talk to you for a minute?"

"I believe you *are* talking to me."

"I just need another minute or two."

He sighed. "As long as it's only for a minute and you don't sit down. I prefer my own company." His British accent was crisp and brusque, and he cupped the Bloody Mary on the table in both hands. He was wearing a navy-blue sport jacket with a white dress shirt, the top button unbuttoned, revealing a clump of chest hair. The hair on his head was short and parted on the left side. His cheeks were ruddy with broken blood vessels.

"All right," I said. "I'll make it quick. I have something of yours." I held up the racket. "This."

"And what is that."

"That," I said, "that is the tennis racket you chucked in Seattle two winters ago."

His eyes stayed on mine. "Is this a joke?"

"No. This is your racket. You lost a match to an Argentine named García and you chucked the racket. When the match ended, you left without ever picking it up. So I went over and picked it up and walked off with it. I've kept it. I—I feel like I've put it to good use. It's—ha-ha!—one of the few things in my life I *have* put to good use. I've used this racket to coach a bunch of kids. For some reason I thought I couldn't get along without it. But I'm returning it to you now. It wasn't right to take it. I—I don't *really* need it."

Gerald Boxton studied me. The lines in his face showed a trace of amusement. He took a long sip of his Bloody Mary. The ice clinked. He made a motion

with his head toward a chair. This was great! He was
inviting me to sit down and join him for a drink. But
he said, "Leave it on the table, then."

"Aren't you going to look at it?"

His eyebrows went up. "Look at it?"

"Yeah. Did you miss it?"

"Did I what?"

"Did you miss it."

He closed his eyes for a second. "I thought about
it night and day. I nearly died of worry."

I smiled shakily. "This—this is a valuable racket,"
I said. "This racket—this racket meant a whole helluva
lot to me, Lord. I know it was wrong of me to take it,
but it meant a lot to me. I'm not saying I was haunted
by guilt or anything. Maybe I should have felt more
guilty, I don't know. I think I *did* feel guilty, only I
just didn't know it. When you're guilty, guilt manifests
itself in weird ways, in how you treat yourself without
even being aware of it."

Boxton picked up his drink, killed it off, and put it
down on the table. He motioned to the waitress for
another. I stood watching him. He cocked his head
and smiled. "You're serious."

"What? Yeah."

He laughed. "My God. Do you honestly think I
care about a tennis racket? Or about your 'guilt' or
how it 'manifests' itself or how you've 'used' the racket
for noble purposes? That is classic. If I didn't insist on

drinking alone, I'd ask you to sit down and have one. Ah well, listen—your two minutes are up. Sorry you have to rush off."

I stared, wavered for a moment. Then I left the racket on the table and walked out.